# FAKE OUT

*Larry Strauss*

*An Original Holloway House Edition*
HOLLOWAY HOUSE PUBLISHING COMPANY
LOS ANGELES, CALIFORNIA

Published by
HOLLOWAY HOUSE PUBLISHING COMPANY
8060 Melrose Avenue, Los Angeles, CA 90046
Copyright © 1994 by Larry Strauss.

This is a work of fiction. Names, characters, places, and incidents
are either the product of the author's imagination or are used fic-
titiously. Any resemblance to actual events or locales or persons,
living or dead, is entirely coincidental.

International Standard Book Number 0-87067-848-5
Printed in the United States of America

Cover photograph by Jeffrey
Cover design by Bill Skurski

*To the Cougars of 94:*

*Tim Daniels, Bobby Parker, Ashley Henkis,*
*Michael Harris, Marcus Clark, John Harris,*
*Michael Williams, Delrick Polly, Charles Ham,*
*Joel Pleasant, Rashien Simpson, Gi'Vonni Joseph*

*Always #1*
*On* and *off the court.*

# FAKE OUT

# Prologue

## *A Player out of Nowhere*

NATURALLY, THIS STORY is not about Gus Anderson Jo, the thirty-five-year-old journeyman power forward/center. Gus's career—his life for that matter—is not the makings of a story, nor even an *Inside the NBA* feature.

Gus's problem, in fact, was that he was now very much *outside* the NBA, good luck having seemed to run out on him.

It hadn't always been that way. Gus's early career was all about being in the right place at the right time. He made the San Antonio Spurs his first season when a guy named Norm Chance tore a ligament. The year after that Gus cleared the final cut on the Cleveland Cavs when Willie Rice got into a contract stalemate.

And that kind of luck put eight NBA seasons on Gus Anderson Jo's trading card—and yet, as he lay prone on the bed of his Eighth Avenue Howard Johnson's room, the telephone receiver dangling from his trembling jaw, the snapping in his brain and the pressure at the back of his throat and the anticipatory chill curling his shoulders made it difficult for Gus not to believe he was a hard-luck case.

"Meyers Agency," answered a young man's voice on the other end of the line.

"This is Gus Anderson Jo. I need to talk to Ray."

"What is this in regards to?"

"I'm a client."

"You *are*?"

Gus felt like informing this smart-ass kid that he had almost single-handedly put Ray Meyers on the sports agent map. Gus was Ray Meyers's first NBA client, signing on after he'd lucked onto the end of the San Antonio bench. Gus, a politically militant honors graduate from Marquette with a degree in African-American history, was influential with a lot of other young black NBA talent—and he convinced two of San Antonio's big-money rookies to sign with Ray Meyers. But Gus refrained from any self-promotion. Instead he used silence to get through the screen this kid was trying to set for Ray.

"What…? What did you say your name was?" the young voice finally asked.

"Gus. Gus Anderson Jo."

"Didn't you retire?"

"Look, punk, I'm not some nine-seven-six sports trivia gig! Now, can I please talk to Ray?"

10

While on hold, Gus tried to get comfortable. The conditioned air in his motel room had the smell of frozen chlorine. It nauseated him, but it was better than the alternative. Last night, when Gus and his Italian girlfriend tried to sleep with the machine off, the humidity was unbearable. Gus kept dreaming about a jazz club he used to frequent in Milan and the Roy Haynes band playing "Autumn in New York," how it used to make him homesick for the States. Then he woke up—in New York, in autumn, swimming in his own perspiration, wishing he was anywhere else.

"This is Ray!" came a speaker-phone voice.

"Huh?" It did not surprise Gus that Ray Meyers no longer considered him significant enough to expend the energy of lifting the receiver—but it still added to his anxiety. He imagined the words he was about to say leaping from the speaker into the air and lingering there.

"Who is this?" Meyers asked.

"It's Gus. Gus Anderson Jo."

"Are you in New York?"

"Yeah…."

"How long?"

"I just got in last night," Gus lied. He and Lucia had arrived from Milan almost a week ago—under the false pretense that Gus had a guaranteed NBA contract. And Gus had, until now, been unable to get Lucia—who distrusted Americans in general and New Yorkers in particular, far enough away to make this call. (She was now, finally, at Bloomingdale's with Gus's Discover Card and an attitude.)

"Weren't you supposed to report to Milan this

month?"

"I'm not playing in Italy this year."

"Oh, shit, Gus. Don't do this to me."

"I want an NBA job."

"Gus, they love you over there…."

"I know," Gus said. There was no denying this—especially since his return to the United States. Gus was now acutely aware of the color of his skin and its implications. Walking down the streets of New York he saw fear and hatred in people's eyes (even his own people did not seem to trust a six-foot-ten black man). In the streets of Milan and Rome and Florence, eyes of respect and admiration and even love followed him everywhere.

"I got you good European dough," Meyers whined. "I know, I know, the lira exchange sucks right now. I tried to get you a currency stipulation, but it was take-it-or-leave-it. I mean, Dominique Wilkins you ain't. They were gonna make Earl Cureton an offer. Shit, Gus, I know you've done a lot for me, but I think we're about even now. Before I got you Milan you was with the Wyoming Whachamacallits in the CBA. Before that you was a pansy for the Globetrotters. Face it, Gus, your best years are ancient history."

"Let me put it another way," Gus clarified. "I *need* an NBA job."

"You need an NBA job," Meyers muttered. "Question is, does any team in the NBA need *you*?"

"I'll try out. I'll go to rookie camp. I've been working out with weights. I bulked up. I'm ready to bang with the millionaires again. I just want one year. I need a year in the NBA to up my pension enough to put me through law school." Gus flexed for the mirror to his right. He tried to be encouraged by the muscle definition—but at the same time he noticed the gray shedding its most recent application of Grecian Formula.

"What can I say, Gus. My guess is your best shot—and it ain't a great shot either—is with the Sacramento Kings. I'll give Donnie a call this afternoon."

"How about New Jersey?"

"What *about* New Jersey?"

"I *have* to play in New Jersey. For the Nets."

"You *have* to? What do you mean you *have* to? I think you been puttin' too much pasta into the wrong orifice, Gus. Nothing *has* to be *any*thing in the NBA. You'll be lucky to get a ten-day contract at the Sacramento rookie camp."

Gus felt a brief and very perverse sense of relief. It's impossible, he told himself. You did your best, Gus. Give it up. Then compulsion took over, stiffened his body, told it: don't move until you get some satisfaction. "New Jersey, Ray. Call New Jersey."

"Why? I want to know why? Why does a guy who wants another season so's he can fatten his pension care whose fuckin' pine he squats on for eighty-two games? Is this some drug thing? Is this about some crack connection you got in Patterson? 'Cause if it is, I'll tell you right now, Gus, I don't know you. You don't exist. You understand?"

"It isn't drugs," Gus said. "It's more serious than that."

"So what the hell is it?"

"It's my kids," Gus said. "They live in Plainfield

13

with my ex-wife. They need a father. I need to see them. I need to be near them. I'm half a man, Ray. Can you help me?"

A long sour sigh, then Meyers groaned: "What am I, a goddamned social worker?"

Gus sighed back. If Meyers wanted to give Gus the shoulder, he'd have to do it the hard way. He'd have to get the lining of his suit a little wet.

"Gus?"

"I'm here."

"Look, I don't know what you want me to do."

Gus said nothing. He waited. He listened for the sound of perspiration on the other end of the line.

"All right, Gus, all right. I'll tell you what. I'll check into it. I'll see what I can do. I think maybe.... I mean, there's a remote possibility is what I'm saying...that I can tack you onto the end of somebody's trade—but I don't know if I can get you any guarantees. And if there's any chance of this happening, it's gonna depend on can I come up with another player."

"What do you mean come up with another player?"

"I think for me to pull this shit off I'm gonna have to invent a player out of nowhere."

# 1

# *Suitcase Full of Dreams*

"WHERE TO?" THE YOUNG taxi driver asked, his cab still bouncing from its sudden stop in front of coach Nick Cruschenctuwitz. "The city?"

"Yeah, the city," answered the coach, as he stood before the Divine Airlines door of the TWA terminal at Kennedy airport. "The Morningside Hotel on One-hundred and Eighteenth Street."

The cabby grimaced, his Adam's apple fluttering. He spun out of his seat, ran around the vibrating grill of his yellow LTD, grabbed the coach's Samsonite, tucking it under his hairy right arm, and, with his left hand, jabbed a key into the trunk lock. Just as the trunk popped open, a short, beefy, no-necked man poked the antenna of a walkie-talkie into the cab driver's back.

"No no no no," he told the cabby. "You got to go through me. This ain't midtown. This the airport."

"What's the problem?" Coach Cruschenctuwitz asked, still standing on the curb.

"Rules is rules," the guy said. He reminded Coach Cruschenctuwitz (who was known throughout the NCAA and sports world as "Captain Crunch") of a particular Big-Eight referee who liked to stop a game—and kill any momentum either team might have—in order to ignite an impromptu three-ring circus on the court just because there was a half-second differential between the two forty-five-second clocks. (As if Captain Crunch would ever allow his team to use more than fifteen seconds per possession in their supersonic transition run'n'gun'n'pound-the-glass offense!)

"Please," the driver said to the man with the walkie-talkie. "I'm off in half an hour. I gotta get the cab back to Fifty-eighth Street. Lemme catch a last fare."

"Fine, no problem, but you gotta go through the dispatcher."

"So who's the dispatcher?" the cabby asked.

"Me."

"So can I have this fare?" the cabby asked.

"You have to wait in line, Scoop."

"I'm askin' you please."

"An' I'm tellin' you no."

"Come on." The driver reminded Crunch of himself arguing with that big-headed Big-Eight ref—and many similar Division-One refs from sea to shining sea.

16

The dispatcher ignored the plea. He waved another taxi over and told Crunch: "Take this cab, sir."

Crunch looked over at the dejected young cabby still holding the Samsonite and asked the dispatcher: "What if I wanna take cab number one?"

"You can't do it."

"You're gonna stop me?"

The dispatcher snorted at Crunch, then pivoted toward the Brillo-haired driver and grabbed Crunch's bag. The driver wouldn't let go. A struggle ensued. The bag lurched into the air. It bounced off the roof of a limousine, then slid beneath the tire of a shuttle bus, which promptly rolled over it, leaving a black tread-mark across the side.

"Sonuvabitch!" Crunch grabbed the dispatcher by the ear, as he had once grabbed that infamous Big-Eight referee—whose name escaped him—but unlike the Big-Eight striped Napoleon (who had merely ejected Crunch from the game), the dispatcher showed Crunch a nickel-plated stun gun.

Crunch let go, backed away, and waited patiently for further instructions.

IT WAS A LONG WAY from Four Corners University in the Arizona, New Mexico, Utah, and Colorado deserts. Crunch's cab—the one that the fascist dispatcher had insisted he ride in—was now on the Triborough bridge, creeping toward a toll booth. A man dressed like a mercenary soldier weaved between the cars selling evening newspapers, flashing the headline at everyone's windshield:

17

# SUBWAY STRIPPER
## MAY HAVE ACCOMPLICE!

Crunch reached into his shirt pocket for a pack of Big Red cinnamon chewing gum, then changed his mind. Big Red was a desert oasis chew, and Crunch was in New York City. This was no place for Big Red. This was no time to be thinking about Four Corners; no time to be thinking about a seventeen-year-old son named Todd, whose every action seemed motivated by a perverse desire to bring misery to his father. This was no time to think about a boy who'd once said he wanted to be just like his dad—a boy who, as a toddler, used to collect things in pairs: a daddy rock and a boy rock, a daddy ball and a boy ball, a daddy tin can and a boy-sized tin can.

This boy, who was the best high-school hoopster in the short book of Four Corners history, had, days ago—despite the intense recruiting efforts of Crunch—given an oral commitment to make his collegiate hardwood house-calls at the University of North Carolina. The boy now even refused to talk to Captain Crunch, as a father or as a coach. But Crunch wasn't about to exhaust any more brain cells on that ungrateful sonuvabitch. He had a more immediate recruiting dilemma to contend with. Crunch crumpled the Big Red pack in his palm and stuffed it into an ashtray of petrified cigarette filters.

He stared out of the taxicab window. In the distance, the island of Manhattan looked like a gigantic cemetery of overcrowded tombstones. Somewhere within that truculent island metropolis was a young man who needed the love and wisdom of Captain Crunch. This young man, a resident of Harlem, had been given an opportunity to acquire a college education and play Division-One basketball under one of the great coaches in the game—if the coach could be so immodest in the presence of his own mind. But basketball was most certainly secondary. *Nothing is more important for a ghetto kid than an education.* Especially this particular ghetto kid who had not attended the last two years of high school due to threats upon his life from gang members in an English composition class.

*Christ!* Crunch wondered, *is he even alive?*

It was now almost two months since Jerome Straughter had been scheduled to report to Four Corners University for the fall quarter and for varsity basketball practice. If he didn't show up within the next few weeks he wouldn't be able to register for the winter quarter and he most certainly would be ineligible to play basketball. Crunch and his staff had been trying to reach Straughter since September. Jerome's telephone number was out of service, with no new number. Mail came back mutilated with stamped postal complaints that no such addressee lived at any such address.

Last week tragedy had struck when Yule McMahon, Captain Crunch's number-four assistant coach, made this very same sojourn to Harlem to try to find Straughter and, during the course of his search, was fatally struck on the head by a car battery dropped from the fifteenth floor of a housing project.

The rest of Captain Crunch's assistants had refused

to go to Harlem, and they had urged Crunch himself not to risk his own life.

"How do you even know the kid is still alive?" his number-one assistant—called "Sheriff" in honor of his previous occupation—had asked.

"I don't," Crunch had admitted. This was in the locker room after practice two days ago. Steam from the showers hung in the air. Soap bubbles spat at them from where two redshirt freshmen were lathering up. "But I gotta try."

"You don't gotta."

"Yes I do," Crunch had said. "This same thing happened back in '73 while you was still in Durango Colorado takin' bribes. I recruited a kid named Clayton Haines from some ghetto in North Philly. He didn't show up for school. Or for practice. I called; the phone had been disconnected. I wrote; the mail came back. So I wrote him off. Six years later the kid shows up. He'd lost his plane ticket and my number and address. He didn't know how to get in touch with me. His family had been evicted from their shack. The city of brotherly love had moved them to a welfare hotel on the south side with no phone. Clayton Haines hit the road. Hitchhiked all the way to Four Corners. Took him six years. Spent two of them in jail for a robbery he didn't commit in someplace called Clyde, Texas.

"*Six years*, man! Spent the last six months with a traveling circus cleaning up after elephants and monkeys and camels so he could get from Odessa, Texas, to Four Corners. Six fucking years. Had barely touched a basketball during that time. Six fucking years. And I was the one who had to tell him it was too late. He could have been an NBA prospect six fucking years earlier, but it wasn't six fucking years earlier. It was six fucking years *later.... Six fucking years!*"

SIX FUCKING YEARS—that was how long it seemed to take to get over the Triborough and across 125th Street, then down Amsterdam Avenue to the Morningside Hotel, a tenement with an old rust-framed red neon sign that sounded like a beehive and a wrinkled banner announcing:

WE HAVE CABLE TV AND ADULT MOVIES.

"This is it?" Crunch asked, apprehensively.

"Morningside Hotel. Hundred Eighteenth an' Amsterdam," said the driver.

"Where's Columbia University?" Crunch asked.

"You want to go Columbia University?"

"I just want to know where it is."

"Two blocks that way, one block right...."

"Three blocks from here?" Captain Crunch's geographic perspective on the world was drawn largely from his knowledge of the locations of Division-One universities. St. Johns was, by this logic, surrounded by Irish Catholic hooligans. Columbia on the other hand, was supposed to be the Ivy League of WASPs and fine dining.

Crunch paid the driver through his bulletproof partition and hauled his bag into the dim hotel lobby strewn with low plastic sofas that resembled rows of green and red blisters. The carpet looked as though it had just been worked over with a lawn mower.

"*Que paso?*" asked an emaciated clerk, staring at a two-inch television.

"Beg your pardon?" the coach asked, taken aback. In Four Corners, the Latin Americans, no matter how bad their English, always made some effort with it. Here in New York, they seemed to expect Crunch to converse in their lingo.

"Wha' can I do *por* you?"

"I have a reservation. Cruschenctuwitz." Crunch had to raise his voice above the music coming from somewhere. Angry trumpets and brazen amplifiers. They kept getting louder, the sounds entering his body through his ears and his spine. He felt his liver start to vibrate.

The clerk—whose eyes each looked in a different direction, neither directly at Crunch—laid out his palm and said, "Thirty-five dollars...."

Crunch handed over seventy dollars, shouted, "I'll be here at least another night," and was handed a tarnished key.

"*Venticinco.*" the clerk said. "Room twenty-five."

Crunch took the key. It felt like a dull razor blade in his hand. He began to smell his own after-shave lotion—Medicated Wild November Forest—which his ex-wife had given him eight years ago. The bottle must have broken during the mayhem at the airport. The music got louder—conga drums and other percussion instruments. Suddenly, a tune emerged from the Latin clamor. Crunch was hearing "Suitcase Full of Dreams" played with a mambo beat.

The coach picked up his suitcase full of broken glass and spilled after-shave and headed for the stairs. He reached the top of the first creaky flight, looked around, and hollered down to the clerk: "Hey, there's no numbers on the doors!"

The clerk hollered back some vile sounding Spanish, then translated: "Fifth door on the left. You can count?"

THE MUSIC HAD NO TROUBLE reaching the second floor. It flourished within the four walls of room 25—and within the nervous system of Captain Crunch. Crunch dropped his bag. He didn't open it. He didn't even want to look at the damage. Collapsing on the bed, feeling the floor beneath the sagging mattress, Crunch leaned toward the television, popped a quarter into its slot, and searched desperately for ESPN.

ESPN—the Captain's old friend, twenty-four hours of sports. Even if it was an event so grotesque as celebrity deer hunting, at least it was something to watch. In Four Corners it knifed through the desolation. Now, here, in Morningside Heights, New York City, ESPN was a refuge of familiarity—a piece of Mom's fudge hidden in a shell casing at the front lines of a war.

He found it! Channel 23: the ESPN minor league baseball scoreboard superimposed upon the end of the Dade County Paraplegic Volleyball Tournament—the winning trio embracing sideways in their wheelchairs; then a beer commercial and an endless *Sports Illustrated* offer; then collegiate basketball: the preseason Great Lakes Cage Classic, already in progress. A chance for Captain Crunch to do some scouting. No, wait. It was his team. They were playing. The Four Corners Posse—in their blood-red visitors' uniforms!

Senior Joe Mudd, the seven-and-a-half foot Ozark center. Raw, but big and intimidating. His long blond hair already dripping with sweat, clinging to his face like the veins of a monster. He'd come a hell of a long way from his days as a spastic freshman with feet of lead.

At power forward, junior Clarance Watson, the six-foot-ten brick shithouse from Oakland. Big, black, and bad—the guy once bench-pressed six pantyless cheerleaders sitting on a chunk of plexiglass—but also he had a soft touch jump shot from inside fifteen feet.

Small forward Lasalle Mack gave Crunch a special amount of joy. Not only did he possess great versatility—could score, rebound, hustle, and play aggressive D—but he was from Pactolus, North Carolina. Captain Crunch had recruited the kid right out from under Dean Smith, coach of the Carolina Tar Heels.

Crunch had nothing personally against Smith—except that Smith's style of coaching was the antithesis of his own. Smith was conservative, old fashioned. He had engineered the most tedious offense in the history of the sport. Smith's offense had once been called—ironically—the "four corners" offense—while at Four Corners University they played slam-bam-candish-feed-swoop, in-your-face, light-'em-up, rip-'em-down entertainment-style, instinct-over-blackboard-and-chalk basketball.

That was the kind of hoop Lasalle Mack wanted to play, and that must have sent a message to the stuffy old conservative brain trust of collegiate basketball. And Crunch's Carolina recruiting coup held added significance now that Crunch's own son Todd had made that oral commitment to the Tar Heels next year, preferring to play for Dean Smith "and get a diploma from a 'real' university" than to lace-up the treads for his own dad.

The off guard on this year's Posse would perhaps prove to be the greatest pure shooter in the history of the game—better than Reggie Miller, better than Larry Bird in his prime or Rick Barry or Adrian Dantley or anyone else. Jonny Never-miss-a-shot Barker, a twenty-year-old Navajo Indian, was phenomenal.

Crunch could still remember his recruiting trip to the southern Utah reservation to see this kid. The miles and miles of dirt roads in a truck without shock absorbers or seatbelts until they came upon a field of rocks. At the center, a mock totem pole with carved heads of the NBA's two most renowned Indians (both of them part Cherokee): NBA legend Connie Hawkins and NBA board-sweeping demon Michael Cage at the top of the pole. A large bottomless bird's nest against a sawed-in-half door. The basketball was authentic, old blackened leather. The kid shot and shot and shot. He had the stroke—with a vengeance. He shot from inside, outside, downtown, uptown; he shot off-balance, he shot from inside a ditch behind the backboard. He did not miss a single shot. Crunch counted: 87 for 87.

And here he was now, in a Posse uniform, number

23, the ritualistic childhood scars of his tribe etched along his wiry arms. Here he was—out on the ninety-four-foot hunk of wood. Double-team anyone else on the Posse and Jonny will burn you and burn you and burn you!

The Posse was deep with talent. They had sharpshooters and frog-legged leapers coming off the bench. They had a role-playing senior named Deontrey Love. What they did not have, at the moment, was a point guard—and without a point guard, Crunch feared, all that talent added up to the unassembled pieces of a Ferrari. The Posse's backup point guard was a freshman from Alabama named Aubry Barnes, a kid with outstanding ability but nerves of jello. Crunch had anticipated that the arrival of Jerome Straughter would inspire Aubry Barnes, but for now, pending that uncertainty, Barnes was a redshirt—along with six-foot-eleven Jo Jo Witherspoon (who needed to beef up his large frame) and two recruits from Podrido, California, whose bodies would take a year or so to fully excrete all the anabolic steroids they'd been given in high school.

No question, the Four Corners Posse was a team of the future—but Crunch was tired of looking forward to next year. This was supposed to be the year they'd all been waiting for. And this was the opening game.

The television screen flashed a close-up of the opposing coach—Bobby Knight of the Indiana Hoosiers. Robert Montgomery Knight. Mr. Conservative himself—except when it comes to throwing chairs. Mr. Fundamentals-first. Bobby "Basketball is

Discipline" Knight, the professor of Xs and Os—the fact that Knight had won three NCAA titles and had won and lost some of the most exciting college games of the last two decades did not impress Captain Crunch, who looked upon Knight as a glorified gym teacher, a coach who did not emphasize (and, in fact, often tried to repress) the poetic flash of a three-on-two fastbreak, the sublime ballet of a 360-degree spin move, the aeronautic bliss of a monster slam.

ESPN flashed the score:

Indiana Hoosiers: 36
Four Corners Posse: 14

The Posse had the ball. Deontrey Love was trying to run the offense. It was anarchy. Center Joe Mudd got a pass at the top of the key, before he could muscle for low post position. Eighteen feet from the bucket, he didn't know what to do with the ball.

"Give it up!" Crunch screamed, his pacing feet defining the sidelines of his tiny room.

Mudd passed the ball to Jonny Never-miss-a-shot, who was standing in the halfcourt circle. Everyone stood still.

"Set a pick!" Crunch pleaded. "Someone set a motherfucking pick!" But no one set a pick—or moved to get a pass. After a four count on the shot clock, Jonny Never-miss-a-shot shrugged and heaved the ball at the basket—as if it were the end of the game. The ball careened off the rim. A brick! Jonny Never-miss-a-shot missed!

The ESPN announcer quipped: "Well, I guess

they'll have to change his name to 'Jonny Never-miss-a-*reasonable*-shot....'"

The Hoosiers caught the long rebound and fast-breaked, then kicked out to a three-point-shooting guard, who drilled it.

"That was a two!" Crunch protested. "His foot was on the line!" Crunch kicked the bedpost and threatened the channel selector with his fist. Losing was hell—but the worst of all fates is to lose on a bad call, to be unjustly defeated by the totalitarian legions of weasel-headed cataract-infested referees who were always telling Crunch to sit down and shut up.

Crunch used this opportunity—this one-way communication with the striped vipers, to vent some frustration. He stood there and called them weasels, then skunks, and kept going until he got to slimey-headed cocksuckers. He talked about their mothers. His satisfaction was transitory. His team kept turning the ball over—unable to make the right passes. Hoosier double teams were stifling, and the open man was always in the wrong place. There was no leadership on the floor.

"Time-out!" Crunch sighed, signaling at the television screen. He thought, *Why didn't I recruit another backup point guard?* The mambo from outside was now the dirge of his soul.

Crunch turned away from the horror on the tube and recalled the scouting report he had read about the point guard he'd recruited—or thought he had: "If you crossed a thoroughbred horse with a gourmet chef and a genie from a bottle you'd have this kid. Jerome Straughter is the second coming of Magic Johnson.

28

Put him on a court with four other guys he has never seen before and he can make them all look like an NBA highlight film. And he never gets tired. He plays fastbreak basketball from noon until dusk every day. He doesn't even have a decent pair of sneakers (which may explain his weak ankles and knees)."

After first reading it, Crunch had immediately had a pair of high-tops Federal-Expressed to the kid—that was back when the kid had an address.

On the TV now, Sheriff, who was coach in Crunch's absence, did call a time-out. Sheriff was a husky, robust man with a deep tan, but as the camera closed in on him, Sheriff was a fat ghost. The players surrounded him in horror. Crunch was overwhelmed with emotion. Hydrochloric acid began to secrete in his gut and vaporize until his entire being burned with remorse. He thought, *How could I have left my team—these young men who look to me for leadership, guidance, and love—in such disarray?* Crunch felt the urge to flee this fleabag hotel and hop the next flight to Port Huron to be with his boys.

Then the game resumed. Mudd broke free under the basket for a rim-flapping dunk—the kind that can instantaneously reverse the momentum of the game. But Deontrey Love didn't see him in time. Mudd had to spin out of the paint to avoid a three-seconds call, and just as he left, Deontrey hurled the ball at the spot where he had been a moment ago. The ball scudded like a meteor into the third row of the stands.

Indiana ball.

Close-up Bobby Knight: he was smiling. Knight never smiles during a game—unless he thinks he's

29

making a statement about how the game should be played.

Captain Crunch whacked the on/off knob until this nightmare shrank to a dot, then he screamed and moaned: "I need my point guard. I can't take a whole season without my point guard!" To be so close—and yet so far—from greatness. "If I have to see Bobby Knight smile one more time...."

Crunch lunged out of bed and stumbled to the window. He opened it, leaned out, and shouted: "Straughter! Jerome Straughter! Where are you?"

But his words were swallowed up by the mambo and the flap of traffic and street chatter—inhaled into the lungs of the city.

# 2

## *Tricky Dick Plaza*

WHEN HE OPENED his suitcase the next morning, Captain Crunch was overwhelmed by the smell. Something had happened to the spilled Medicated Wild November Forest overnight. It had combined with some chemical in the suitcase or in Crunch's clothes, and it had fermented into a substance similar to dog urine. Crunch opened the window and held his nose while he plucked chips of glass from the collars of his shirts and the pockets of his pants, then selected what he would wear today—beige polyester slacks and a brown and white striped cotton shirt.

At the desk in the hotel lobby was a short white lady with a large mole that stood erect like a nipple on her bloated cheek. "*Que paso?*" she asked.

"I'm English speaking."

"Good for you."

"I need a taxicab."

"Go find one." She pointed toward the door. "Try Broadway. It's that way."

"Thank you."

The lady winced, sniffed hard. "You got animals up in your room?"

The street was quiet, or seemed so without the atomic mambo of last night. Across Amsterdam Avenue a pair of black men were changing the oil of a double-parked car. One man was smoking a cigar; the other man was blowing on a hot meatball sandwich.

Crunch turned the corner and walked until he found Broadway. There was a herd of yellow cabs heading toward him. He waved to them. One pulled over. The white driver had a nose the shape of a boat sail. "Where to?" he asked.

The coach showed him an index card on which was written the last known address of Jerome Straughter: 35 West 129th Street, apartment 2D, then he pulled back his arm, which was almost torn out of its socket as the cab screeched away.

Crunch waved to some more yellow cabs. Again, one pulled over and again the address repelled the driver.

This happened three more times.

Finally, a red, black, and green taxi stopped for Crunch. The driver, a black man with freckles and a ponytail, commanded: "Get in, man. I'll take you there."

"Where?"

"Wherever you goin'."

"How do you know where I'm going."

"I don't. What I'm sayin, brah, I will take you to d'muh-fuckin place where them yellow-checkered imperialist mothafuckas are afraid to go."

Crunch handed him the index card.

"No problem."

Crunch opened the door and slid into the sheepskin backseat. The cab screeched into the flow of traffic.

"They think Harlem just a lot of junkies and pimps an' uneducated ignorant slave apes swingin' from fire escapes an' barbecuing pigs in the streets an slicin' watermelon on the rooftop...."

Crunch raised his eyebrows. He started to nod but was afraid the man would suppose he was agreeing with those bigoted assumptions. Actually, Crunch wasn't sure what to expect when he arrived in Harlem.

"Wha'chew doin stickin' your white nose in Harlem anyway, man?"

"I'm looking for a young man named Jerome Straughter. You wouldn't happen to know where he is...?"

"You with the FBI?"

"I'm a basketball coach."

The driver nodded suspiciously and stopped for a red light. "You lookin' for some hood rat so you can exploit his ass...."

"I want to help him get an education."

"In what? The economics of oppressing a people by enriching a select few for a minstrel show on the playing field, kickin' a football, chuckin' a baseball,

33

shootin' a basketball?"

Crunch tried to keep his cool. *Who cares what this fuckin' cab driver thinks?* Crunch did not want to further upset the man behind the wheel in whose hands he'd entrusted his safety. But the stuff about minstrel shows demanded a reply.

"I take good care of my players," Crunch said. "I encourage them to learn subjects that will better them in the world whether or not they make the pros. Black or white. It don't matter to me. They're all the same to me. Just pieces of clay I try to mold into fine young men. I love my players no matter what they are. I'm like a father to them. I hear any racial shit in my locker room I'll kick the living shit out of that boy! Everyone's equal on my team."

"Maybe the brothers don't want your paternalistic morality."

"What?"

"Just because the white man finally decides to be humane toward the Afro-American, does that assume that the Afro-American is ready—has been waiting anxiously his whole chained-up life—to embrace whitey?"

"That ain't what I said," Crunch protested.

"Maybe the young athlete in question does not want your white racist college education."

"Education is the only way these kids are going to rise up out of these slums."

"So you would encourage the young and talented African Americans to abandon their brothers and sisters for the white man's colleges and country clubs, leaving the ghettos and their inhabitants to rot?"

"That ain't what I said."

"Are you offering scholarships to every eighteen-year-old in Harlem?"

"It ain't up to me alone."

"Can I have a scholarship to your school?" the driver asked.

"Can you fill the lane on a fastbreak?"

The driver's laugh was deep and rich. "How many black people can afford to buy a ticket to see your team play?"

"There aren't any black people at Four Corners U—except for the basketball and football teams."

The driver's laugh slowed to a derisive snort. He swerved to avoid a drunken pedestrian, then turned a corner. Crunch looked around. He supposed they were in Harlem now. Everyone was a shade of brown.

"Man, you smell like dog piss," the driver said, then added, without looking at Crunch, "See what your college education gonna do for this?" As if to punctuate his question, he slammed on the breaks, jerking the coach forward.

Through the cab window, Crunch saw a row of charred buildings wrapped in shattered glass and scrap lumber. Crunch did not move from his seat.

"We're here, Mr. Coach. This the place you wanted to go."

"There's no one here."

"Oh, I'm sure you'll find someone around here—or someone will find you...."

Crunch reached into his wallet to pay for the fare. "Maybe you oughtta wait a minute for me," he said.

"Maybe I *oughtta*?"

"Maybe you should."

"*Should*?"

"Maybe, if you would be so kind, you might take it upon yourself to wait a minute for me."

Crunch slid out of the the red, black, and green taxi and closed the door. As he stepped away from the curb, the driver zoomed away, leaving an eerie quiet.

Crunch removed Jerome Straughter's last known address from his pocket and matched it up with the grimy numbers above one of the boarded-up doorways of one of the burned-out tenement skeletons. Then he climbed to the top of its stoop, as if more might be revealed at a higher altitude.

More was not revealed. Just a sheet of splinters blocking entry into this giant cube of hell. Either Jerome Straughter was killed in a fire or simply driven into the streets. Captain Crunch's staff had contacted the city of New York on many occasions to determine whether the kid and his mother were relocated (and if so, where to), but always they were told that no such people existed in the official records.

Crunch turned from the decaying plywood barricade and looked out at the street. An elderly woman pushed a cart of groceries. A shoeless man strutted toward her, swinging a dented bowling ball in one hand. The two people passed each other without incident.

Crunch sat down. If he'd had a smoking habit he would have reached for some variety of tobacco. He wished he had a piece of Big Red chewing gum to help start the motors in his brain. He did not know where to go or what to do next. He heard a sudden

blast of shouting from within the gutted tenement—
two men yelling simultaneously about "snow" and
"dirt" and "shit" and "paybacks dat's a muh-fucka"
and heard grunts and groans and fisticuffs—and
Crunch decided it was time to leave, though he still
had no idea where he was headed.

He hurried down the stoop and tried to seem casual, walking quickly toward the nearest corner. He
passed a vacant lot of dense weeds with a pair of rusted automobile bodies lying upside down like huge
sunbathing turtles. A brown dog charged from behind
one car. Before Crunch could flinch, the animal was
upon him. Crunch turned. Two other mongrels, one
spotted, the other white—though caked with filth—
were at his feet, snarling. Their teeth were cracked
and jagged. Their eyes sparkled demonically in the
sunlight. Crunch felt teeth grasping his shins. He
kicked and reached down with coiled fists, but suddenly the dogs mellowed. All three calmly sniffed the
legs of his pants as if sampling the bouquet of a wine.
Then two of them, the males, lifted their legs and uri-
nated on his pant legs and the toe boxes of his loafers.

In a way, Captain Crunch was relieved. He now
had an immediate objective, an intended destination:
a clothing store.

WAS THIS THE RENOWNED Harlem boutique in
which, sometime during the 1980s, then heavyweight
champion Mike Tyson had punched the contender
Mitch "Blood" Green as both men browsed the leather
jackets at 4:30 one morning? Captain Crunch was
dying to know—think of all the conversational play

he could get out of that—but he was not anxious to ask anyone. At least not until he had shed himself of the canine-scented clothes and established to all creatures of Harlem that he was a human being and not a tree.

The metal awning outside—from which some prankster had hung a pair of soleless shoes and a teeth-marked apron—bore the name, "Kim's Fashions."

Inside, Crunch found a rack of Dockers and selected a green pair. Crunch, who had always secretly wanted to drape himself in something loud, discovered a pile of florescent fishnet sleeveless shirts and grabbed a metallic red. Transparent socks and two-tone Adidas high-tops made the coach a neon wonder.

*When in Harlem,* Captain Crunch thought, sauntering toward the fortified cash register. "Where's your garbage?" he asked, holding his old duds at arms length.

A Korean man in a sweat-stained "Atlantic City" T-shirt held up a pail and helped the coach stuff the urine soaked threads in with yesterday's cigarette butts. "That cash or credit card?"

Crunch lifted some plastic out of his wallet and slid it across the counter. He felt lighter. The after-shave and urine on his pants and shirt and socks and shoes must have weighed five or ten pounds. Crunch leaned on the counter and waited for his credit to be verified. He tapped his foot to the soulful rhythm coming out of the store's hi-fi speakers. He tried to really dig it. To get into it. To orient himself, get in step, to feel the pulse—but the melodious sounds turned out to be

38

the jingle of a local E-Z credit "we-take-Medicare-and-Medicaid" dental clinic, and that left Crunch with a sour taste in his mouth.

He stood still, as if attached to the back of the cash register, and focused his eyes straight ahead. Behind the counter was the usual framed dollar bill, Norman Rockwell bank calendar, a big sign warning "SHOPLIFTERS WILL BE CANED," and a photograph of a young black man with his arm around a Korean girl. The black man looked awfully familiar. At first Crunch thought it might actually be Mike Tyson or Mitch "Blood" Green—but the young man did not look that bulky or psychotic. It took a good minute for the coach to realize he was looking at a photograph of his prized point guard, Jerome Straughter.

"You know him?" Crunch asked the Korean man when he swung back around with a credit verification number.

"Signature and phone number, please."

Crunch signed and numbered the rectangle of commerce and pointed again to the photograph. "Do you know that guy?"

The merchant looked. "My niece. She gone back to Korea."

"The guy. What about the guy?"

"Her boyfriend. What you expect in this neighborhood—all black people..., except for Puerto Ricans...." He gave Crunch a cockeyed glance. "What you doin' here?"

"Looking for that guy in the picture."

"I don't know," the Korean said. His tone was

sharp, staccato, and sounded hostile—though the coach wasn't sure if it was meant to be. "Just her boyfriend. She back in Korea...." The Korean said something else that sounded like "hair farm." Or was it "*heir* farm?"

Crunch was curious as hell but didn't want to get sidetracked. "The guy," Crunch persisted. "Do you know where he is?"

"He live around here."

"I know. But where?"

"He play basketball. Very good."

"I know. He's my fucking point guard!"

"You want your carbons?" The Korean had peeled away the layers of the credit card form and was now offering Crunch his sheet in a sandwich of filthy blue carbon.

"No thank you."

"Try the playground. He like to play basketball."

"What playground?"

"Playground. Where they shoot the ball in the ring...." The Korean crumpled the carbons and hook-shot them into his wastebasket. "Try Dick Plaza."

"Huh?" Crunch asked.

"Tricky Dick Plaza," The Korean said. "Richard Nixon Housing Project. Five block that way up Lennox Avenue."

The five-block walk to the Nixon Projects was, for Captain Crunch, endless. He encountered a man with no legs sleeping in a gutter beneath a sign asking: "Please don't set me on fire." He passed children playing jump rope and hopscotch and freeze tag, and a seven-foot Jamaican swinging a curtain rod—and everyone seemed to be staring at Crunch, eyeing him like he had no business on their street, like he must be crazy or a cop or a landlord or somebody up to some kind of no good.

Four brick buildings that once had been orange, now a kind of tearful rust color, constituted the Richard M. Nixon Housing Project. Connecting the four towers was a series of cemented paths, some receding lawns, some pitiful trees. At the far corner of this public housing landscape, a playground.

Crunch approached this fenced-off sector of jungle gyms, handball walls, and basketball courts. It was vacant. No children on the swings. A closer look: no swings. They'd been decapitated from their fixture. The handball courts were ablaze with layer upon layer of graffiti. The cement slab was cracked in some places, shattered in others. Weeds broke through the surface. But still the coach couldn't believe that no one was playing basketball. He'd heard that New York hoopsters will play under any conditions: rain, snow, ice, wind. What were a couple of weeds? Then he looked up. There were four backboards of orange perforated metal. Not one of them had a rim on it.

There were no baskets!

The sight of a backboard raped of its hoop twisted Crunch's insides, not only because it defiled the game of round ball, but because this vision of rimless courts suggested an overwhelming hopelessness. This, after all, was the ghetto: an unfortunate place to have to start out in life, Crunch knew. But there were supposed to be ways out, among them the celebrated: play basketball, get a college scholarship, make the pros, or at least become educated enough to sell computer supplies—get the hell out of the slums long enough to start to get the slums out of you. And there they were, four ghetto backboards on the playground court—and no fucking baskets.

Crunch walked toward the backboards, until he could look straight ahead without having to see them. That was when he saw the lone figure, sitting on a rotting bench, reading a book.

Having lived in the desert for so many years, Crunch's instinct was to assume he was seeing a mirage. But this was New York City—where many things *seem* like a mirage but are actually quite real. There really was a young black man with a shaved head and he really was sitting on that bench—and he looked startlingly like Jerome Straughter.

Crunch stood still for a while, afraid that as he got closer the resemblance would fade. He wanted to at least pretend he'd found his treasure, at least for the moment. Then he bravely moved forward.

The resemblance did not fade. It got stronger. The young man heard Crunch's footsteps and looked up, and Captain Crunch joyously raise a fist. "Straughter!"

"What?"

"It's you!"

The young man sized Crunch up, as if checking a used car for scratches and dents. "Do you know me?"

"Do I know you?" Crunch guffawed, and laid a healthy slap on the back of the young man who, without rising, flexed his body into a quasi-karate stance.

"It's me, Jerome; it's Captain Crunch!"

"Crunch? You're that coach—from that college."

"Forgot what I looked like?"

"Yeah."

"Well, I sure as hell haven't forgotten what *you* look like!" Crunch extended his hand. The young man, no longer tensed with hostility, gave it a shake. "You're my main man. I came all the way here to New York City to find your ass, and I knew I would because the Four Corners Posse is a team of destiny, son. And you're their leader. Ain't you a little excited?"

"No.... I mean, yeah." The kid seemed dizzy, like there wasn't enough blood in his head at the moment. "I just can't believe you're here," he said, his face aglow—a stale plum turned ripe again.

Captain Crunch reached down and grabbed his player under the armpits and crushed him with an embrace. His player hugged him back. Crunch was overwhelmed by his own emotions. This whole nightmare—from the riff at the Kennedy Airport taxi stand to the nationally televised humiliation at the hands of the Bobby Knight Hoosiers to the militant cab driver to the attack of the pissing mongrels—it would all be worthwhile now.

Forget the ecstasy of fastbreak poetry—that was to come once they returned to Four Corners. This was the sweet creamy filling of life, right here, this moment right here: the bonding of player to coach, the milk of wisdom beginning its flow into the mouth of raw talent!

"What happened?" Crunch asked his player.

"I lost my plane ticket."

"Why didn't you call?"

43

"I lost your number. It got burned up with everything else. We had a fire."

"I know. Did you get hurt?"

"No, I'm all right."

"That's good."

"I can't believe you're here." Straughter's voice was the resurrected spirit of Clayton Haines. *Six fucking years!* echoed inside the coach's brain—and he started to weep uncontrollably. He let it pour out a while, then became self-conscious and tried to distract himself from his emotions. He reached down and picked up the book Straughter had been reading. "What are you reading?"

"Nothing," Straughter mumbled.

"Who's Gray?"

"Huh?"

"The name on the book says *Gray's Anatomy.*"

"Some dude."

"It's a pretty thick book," Crunch said, impressed. He'd never seen a basketball player read anything that dense before and wanted to say so, but he noticed that this discussion about the book was making the young man nervous, so instead he said, "Hey, Straughter. I want you to know that I'm very happy to see you're not just coming to Four Corners because of your basketball abilities. We want you to get an education and become a better individual."

That seemed to put Straughter at ease for the moment. The young man's smile expanded until his ears seemed to have to move out of the way. Crunch smiled back, thinking: *I'd better still get him those answers to the SAT!*

# 3

# *Weaknesses*

"HOW SOON DO WE GO?" Straughter asked, picking up his book and tucking it under his arm.

"Tomorrow morning. First thing. I've got two open tickets and a former player who's high up with Divine.... I just mention his name at the check-in and we're on—even if they have to bump someone off.... Divine, that's an airline," the coach explained, hoping he didn't sound condescending.

"What time should I meet you?"

Crunch laughed. "I didn't come all this way to let you out of my sight. For the next twenty-four hours I'm your shadow. I've got a room at the Morningside Hotel. You can have the bed. I'll sleep on the window ledge." Still consumed with a galvanic lust for his point guard, Crunch leaned over and kissed Straughter on both cheeks.

"Eat your friggin' heart out, Dean Smith!" he hollered. "Wait till we play you next time, Bobby Knight!"

Straughter frowned, slumped his shoulders, and exhaled with exasperation.

"Hey, kid, I kiss all my players. There's nothing, you know... weird gonna happen. I love you guys the way a man loves his dog!"

"Uh-huh...."

"No, wait, I didn't mean...."

"I understand," Straughter said, "but nevertheless I'd like to spend my last night with my girlfriend."

"So bring her along."

"And my mama?"

"Why don't we go to your place?"

ENTERING BUILDING NUMBER 3 of the Nixon Housing Project, Captain Crunch had to adjust his eyes from the sunny outdoors to the dim lobby. There were light fixtures on the ceiling, but the frosted bulbs were all smashed—despite the metal cages around them. The elevator was an ascending box of gloom, its only illumination from the tiny filaments inside the few buttons that had not been looted. The ninth-floor hallway was a dark tunnel strewn with the glass dust of shattered florescent sticks. On someone's door hung a large poster that had been so defiled with ink, paint, and saliva that only the words "VOTE FOR" were decipherable.

Straughter's door was at the other end of the hallway, near a barred window facing uptown toward the Harlem River, the zigzag of bridges and the smoke-stacks and baby food billboards along the South Bronx shore. All looked calm. Captain Crunch sucked in a relaxed breath.

Inside the Straughter residence unmolested light prevailed. A cheerful living room with plastic-covered furniture, a rainbow of flowering plants, walls crowded with velveteen religious depictions.

"Have a seat, Coach. Can I get you a drink?"

"I'm fine." Crunch sat down and thumbed through a magazine called *The New England Journal of Medicine.*

"I'll be right back." And Straughter disappeared behind a closed door.

Captain Crunch put down the *New England Journal,* unable to comprehend any of its contents, perplexed that a high-school dropout would be reading such highbrow stuff. Closing his eyes, Crunch concentrated on the sounds through the closed door—first mumbling, then expressions of excitement, then a mournful howl. Soon, Straughter emerged with a slender young black woman. Her hair was braided and wrapped around her head like the brim of a hat. Her face was small but expansive, her fluffy cheeks like toasted marshmallows.

Crunch stood up to greet her. "Jerome's girlfriend?"

No, The woman shook her head.

"She's my mother," the young man said. "Her name is Patricia...."

Crunch beamed up his recruitment charm, his living-room suave. He kissed her hand. "Pleased to meet

47

you, Patricia."

"That's my name…. I mean…." She grimaced with embarrassment. "I apologize. I'm kind of nervous. I've never met a coach before."

"Well, there's nothing to be afraid of—long as you don't put on a striped jersey."

Soon Straughter's girlfriend arrived. She was tall and her body was thick and sensual. She wore a uniform that spelled out the words "Woolworth's" on the right breast and "Tiffany" on the left. She eyed Captain Crunch with the same contempt that most of Harlem had bestowed upon him all morning.

"This is my coach, Captain Crunch," Straughter said and then quickly dragged her into a back room. When they emerged, Tiffany was wiping tears and blowing her nose. She extended her hand to Crunch and they shook. She said, gulping: "Take good care of Sweety-D."

"Who?"

"Sweety-D…. Dee…."

Straughter stepped behind her, his arms hugging her waist. "That's my nickname, Coach."

"Dee?"

"Yeah, Dee."

"For defense?" Crunch asked.

"Yeah, Dee for defense…."

Crunch nodded—though his scouting report on Jerome Straughter had mentioned that defense might actually be a liability. "Don't you worry about your boy here," Crunch said. "I take care of all my kids."

He thought about the girl's concern periodically for the rest of the night. Every time he heard glass breaking outside or heard a wild scream or dogs snarling or a loud boom that might be a gunshot or heard fire engines or smelled smoke, he wondered how anyone from here could be worried about someone's safety when that someone was *leaving* this place.

Captain Crunch slept sideways on the larger of the two plastic-covered sofas. He woke up with the after-taste of a dream in which he was suffocating in a ziplock bag. Last night's smell of arson was now the scent of ashes. Crunch could also whiff coffee and scrapple and toasting wheat. He was delighted. His nerves felt parched; his psyche was low on oil. It need-ed some egg yolks, some butter, some sausage lard.

Breakfast portions were small, and Crunch ate even less than he was allotted, but he felt filled up and lubricated just the same. He wanted to pay for the meal and the rest of the hospitality, but he knew from his own meager childhood in an unincorporated dis-trict of Strep County, Oklahoma, that such gestures can be an insult to poor people, so instead he dropped a twenty-dollar bill between the cracks of the sofa cushions he'd slept on.

That would also cover the hot water and soap need-ed for his shower and the use of whatever shaving equipment was available. As it turned out the only shave cream in the tiny bathroom was egg shave, a putrid smelling medicated lather many of his black players over the years had had to use due to their propensity for facial ingrown hairs. Strangely, the stuff didn't smell so bad to Captain Crunch when it cov-ered his own face. And he didn't need a razor; the stubble fell out with a tingle. Wiping his face with a frayed hand towel, he realized that, despite not using his Medicated Wild November Forest after-shave, his skin irritation had not flared up at all. The egg shave worked on his own pink cheeks—and that afforded the coach a warm sense of commonality with Jerome Straughter, a feeling he'd most likely need to get through the morning.

After he combed his thinning brown hair, got dressed, and stared himself down in the bathroom mirror, Crunch stepped through the living room arch and into the discomfort of tearful goodbyes.

It embarrassed the coach to see his player crying in the slender arms of his mother and bracing his head against the bosom of his girlfriend. Crunch reeled into the bathroom but couldn't escape the sound of weeping. He felt responsible. That he was granting the kid the opportunity of a lifetime did not make up for the fact that he was tearing him from these two lovely ladies.

Crunch sat on the toilet lid, closed his eyes, and covered his ears. This display of emotion frightened him. He recalled 1977, the year he almost recruited Earvin "Magic" Johnson of Lansing, Michigan. If there ever was a player who exemplified the style of ball Captain Crunch taught, coached, breathed, it was Magic Johnson. Crunch had Magic signed, sealed, and delivered, but then the kid got homesick—before he'd even left home—and enrolled instead at Michigan State. Crunch grew annoyed by the prospect that Straughter might also allow himself to be ruled by his heart.

*—I'm giving that kid what he needs! An education!*

*GROW UP, STRAUGHTER! I'm your new family.... The Posse is your new family. These people holding onto you right here are just relatives!*

Captain Crunch thought about his ex-wife, Judy—now married to Ed Clover, an NBA referee!—and his son, Todd. Goddamn, was Crunch ever proud of that boy. An honor-roll student and a high-school all-state first team in four states! Crunch had bestowed upon the boy everything he knew and felt about basketball, and the kid had responded with hard work and devotion—and whatever it took to grow to be six-foot-six tall (Crunch believed Todd had somehow willed himself to that height)—and Todd was a sacrificial competitor but also a brave loser (on those few occasions) and, above all, a decent human being....

*So why in the hell does he want to play for Dean Smith over his own father?*

In an undaunted rage, the coach released his ears, unafraid to hear the sobs from the other room. Those tears and moans were nothing more than the standard issue wail of the human spirit, the normal condition of the homo sapiens. *Man comes out crying and the best he can do most of the time is to hide those tears, to suppress them with cheap thrills, expensive thrills, ambition, laughs, alcohol, drugs, and the donut family of foods. Music and paintings and other so-called "artistic expressions" make that wail into something less annoying to look at or hear. They are wallpaper.*

But basketball.... Basketball, when played the right way, transcends the sob of existence! It annihilates it—at least until some goddamn blind referee starts calling ticky-tack fouls or bogus three-seconds....

*Straughter won't be crying once he gets on the court, center stage at the Four Corners Corral! The fans. The attention. He'll forget about his mother. He'll have girls throwing themselves at him—black girls, white girls, Mexican girls, Japanese girls, Apache girls....*

Confident of his composure, Captain Crunch rose from the toilet lid and strutted into the living room—and felt worse than he had before.

Tiffany was, at that moment, telling Straughter, "Now you be true now," and kissing him, then caressing a heart-shaped piece of costume jewelry around his neck that matched one around hers. Straughter's mother looked away from the lovers and winked at the coach with a sad smile. Crunch consulted his watch. "Say, how long does it take to get to the airport?"

Straughter's mother gazed back at him in a way that suggested she'd never been to the airport. "An hour," she said. "Two hours. When's your plane take off?"

"One o'clock."

"Better hurry then."

But neither the mother nor the coach made a move to terminate the amorous embrace of the other two people in the room.

Crunch felt ruminations somewhere within his intestines. He thought about the big-city traffic that stood, like a great bed of lava, between them and Divine Airlines. He tried to diminish the profundity of the lovers embrace before him. He remembered the snapshot on the wall of Kim's Fashions. In the photo,

Straughter had his arm around a pretty Korean girl. How many other girls did this playboy have? Heck, he'd fit right in on the Four Corners Posse.

"Well," Crunch said, apropos nothing. "That about does it. It's now or never, son." Crunch immediately regretted that phrase, afraid of what choice the boy would make in light of this ultimatum. "Christmas vacation's just around the corner," he added.

Straughter and the girl disengaged from each other, except for their fingers.

"Where your bags?" Crunch asked. He'd carry them so his point guard could have his million-dollar hands free.

Straughter looked down at a single cloth suitcase, red plaid on the front and back and gray along the edges. The seams were partially frayed, and places were patched with what looked like dish towels. The handle was held on with a shoelace.

"That's it?" Crunch asked. "That's your only bag?"

Straughter nodded.

Crunch picked up the bag by its precarious handle. He gave it the once-over. He hoped to God that it didn't burst open from the brutality of airline baggage handlers. There was no more pathetic sight than a hemorrhaging suitcase revolving around the luggage rack, its contents spread across the rubber belt for all the world to see. Crunch thought about stopping by the Morningside Hotel. He'd paid for the room in advance and didn't care much about the clothes and other personal effects he'd left there—most of which were saturated with Medicated Wild November Forest—but Crunch would like to have been able to collect his Samsonite so he could let this kid use it.

By the time they'd gotten downstairs, however, and said goodbye and hugged and shaken hands and hugged again and found a gypsy cab willing to carry them to Kennedy airport and then hugged and said goodbye again, it was 11:30—too late to stop anywhere for anything.

It was a five-minute ride through narrow Harlem streets—past a massive grid of fire escapes, a collage of drying laundry hanging over vacant lots and street-corner domino games—and then they were on the Triborough bridge. The traffic taunted Crunch. At one point it came to a complete halt, suggesting not only that they would miss their plane but that they would spend the rest of their lives beneath the New Jewel Avenue exit sign. Then the road freed up, the cab driver zoomed up to sixty miles per hour—for about one hundred feet—then had to come to a screeching halt, like a four-on-one fastbreak without a middle man.

The coach and his new player didn't say much to each other for most of the ride. At one point Straughter took a magazine out of his pocket and started to read. Then, self-consciously, he closed the pages and rolled the periodical into a tube.

"It's all right," Crunch told him. "Go ahead and read. It ain't rude. I don't mind. I want you to read. I think it's great that you're expanding your intellect...."

"Thanks," Straughter said, but he did not open the magazine.

"How *are* your three Rs anyway, son?"

"Excuse me?"

"Reading, 'riting, and 'rithmatic...."

The young man shrugged.

"I mean, I know you didn't finish high school but as far as I'm concerned that don't mean squat. Everybody knows high-school curriculum is racially biased. The main thing is you got a good head on your shoulders and you have the desire to do good in school once you get the chance."

"I will."

"I know you will. But just out of curiosity, you ever heard of a test called the SAT?"

"I got a twelve-hundred...."

"You *what*?" If that were true Crunch might consider going to church this Sunday.

The young man stammered. Crunch's sudden show of excitement seemed to frighten him. "Ain't that the high-school equivalency test in New York State? They said just a few more points and I'd have passed."

"No," Crunch said, unable to conceal his disappointment. "The SAT is a *college* entrance exam. You'll have to take one. But don't worry. We'll help you study and give you the answers, and if you think you need it, we can set you up with a hearing aid during the test and feed you the answers. It's just that, well, there is the chance you could get caught cheating and we'd all be hangin' by our short hairs, so, I mean, if you think there's any way you can pass the test without help, just let me know."

"I think I can, coach."

"You sure now?" Crunch asked, his innards trembling with the dread of that hell of coach's hells: NCAA academic probation.

"All I need is a chance to prove myself," the kid said.

"You'll have plenty of chances to prove yourself on the ninety-four-foot hunk of wood."

"But I think I can pass that SAT test."

"Are you positively sure, though?"

"You just said if I thought there was any way I could pass without help...."

"I know what I said.... And I meant it.... I'm just nervous as hell, that's all. Boy..., son..., did you know I almost recruited Magic Johnson?"

"No, I didn't know that."

"Well, I did. I had him in the palm of my offensive scheme."

"What happened?"

"Problems with the SAT. I can't go into details. Let's just say Michigan State played him a hell of a lot smarter than I did."

Crunch lifted his watch up in front of his face and gasped. It was 12:40. "How much longer?" he asked the driver, whose face Crunch never did get a clear view of—just his ears which were hairy like the fungal growth on a russet potato.

The driver shrugged. "Five, ten, twenty minutes."

"Which one?"

Raffi Packtanian—Crunch read the name off the plastic-framed license over the glove box—did not answer, but Raffi did make an incredible lane change between two Getty petroleum tankers and then swerved in front of a cement truck as if to show the coach that he was trying his best to transcend the gridlock.

Soon Crunch could see the airport; the horizon was a shooting gallery of airplanes slanting upward and downward. Captain Crunch checked his watch again: *ten minutes left. A big deficit to make up. Crunchtime and no remaining time-outs!*

The coach did what he always did in that situation—on or off the court. He prayed like hell, then crossed his fingers and sweated and made his heart pound as loud as it could in his chest and throughout his bones, and he coached from the sidelines: "Right lane. You got an opening, man. Right lane. Nice move, pretty move.... Swing left. All right, baby, we're movin'...."

They were moving quite fast now. Crunch could smell the sweet airport diesel fumes of victory. They were almost to the ramp marked TWA, N.Y. Air, Piedmont, Divine Airlines.

"Come on, Raffi.... You can do it, Raffi...." The most rewarding and frustrating thing a coach does is watch his players out there on the floor, helpless to guide them, only able to encourage from the bench. "We got em, Raffi. We're gonna make it! Yeah!"

They arrived. The cab stopped in front of the Divine door. Crunch slapped a pair of twenty-dollar bills in Raffi's calloused palm. He grabbed Straughter and the sad suitcase and bolted inside the terminal— and joined the end of the security check line.

There were fifty-seven people ahead of them, including five reggae musicians with guitars and steel drums. The lead singer, whose dreadlocks were like darkened cauliflower, was threatening to sue the airport if his band missed their gig in Little Rock; the head of security, a severe Polish woman wearing an aluminum necklace, yawned back at him. Captain Crunch scanned the terminal for a television screen of arrivals and departures—and watched their flight, Divine 658 to Albuquerque, start to blink—then he saw their plane, a 727, speed past the thirty-foot window and soar into the clouds.

An unfriendly ticket agent named Joy informed the coach that the next Divine flight to Albuquerque was not for twenty-four hours, but a competing airline would be flying there from La Guardia airport in approximately three hours.

"You hungry?" Crunch asked Straughter. The coach had a powerful craving for something with a rancid tang beneath a ketchupy wallop. "I thought we might stop at the TWA cafeteria and get some burgers."

Straughter offered no resistance. In addition to their burgers, the coach and his player shared a bowl of onion rings and a slice of cornbread that some misguided food service worker had spread white icing on. Then they went next door to the gift shop. Crunch bought himself some Big Red gum, some metallic tasting breath mints, the latest *Sports Illustrated*, and then bought Straughter a new piece of stiff vinyl luggage.

"Thanks a lot, coach," the young man said outside the gift shop, as together they transferred the contents of Straughter's dilapidated suitcase.

"Don't mention it," Crunch said.

Straughter smiled.

"I'm serious. Don't mention this to anyone. This was not a gift. You bought this yourself with your own money. Same goes for the food. I paid for the cab and the plane tickets, but your personal shit came out of your own pocket."

"Why?"

"NCAA recruiting regulations."

Straughter threw his head back. "You tellin' me if I was starvin' to death you couldn't buy me a meal?"

"I couldn't even buy you a Baby Ruth."

"If I was freezing to death and you bought me a blanket…?"

"The Four Corners basketball program could get the death penalty for two to five years."


OUTSIDE AT THE TAXI stand Captain Crunch recognized the militarized dispatcher who had, days ago, aimed a Saturday night special at his nose. "There must be a bus that goes to La Guardia," Crunch said to his player.

There was. It was crowded with nuns, a drunken team of Canadian rugby players, and assorted bureaucrats and business people. The vehicle smelled like a wallet that had spent too much time in a hind pocket.

Straughter fell asleep. Crunch watched the rise and fall of the kid's chest nervously, as if he might stop breathing, go into a coma, and never be able to run the Four Corners Posse offense. After a while, Crunch relaxed. Then, as they approached the La Guardia highway exit, he saw a playground—a game of sandlot basketball—and was overcome with excitement. He thought: *I've got the best goddamn player in this entire great metropolis—perhaps in the whole god-*

*damn country—and he's coming with me, back to Four Corners!*

Crunch couldn't wait. "Wake up, kid," he urged as the bus stopped at their terminal and belched open its doors.

The kid woke up; Crunch rushed him off the bus and inside the terminal. He shoved some change into a coin operated locker and slid the new suitcase inside, then looked around. "How the hell do we get out of here?" he wondered aloud.

"Ain't this the airport?"

"Yeah, but we've still got two-and-a-half hours."

"Where are we going?"

"We're going to play some basketball."

This seemed to concern the kid.

"What's the matter?"

"I ain't familiar with this area. This is Queens, man. They got a different style of ball in Queens. That's what I heard."

Crunch laughed. "They got a ball and a hoop of approximately ten feet."

"I don't feel well, coach."

"Just one game…. I don't think I can wait another day to see you play."

Straughter just stared off into the distance for a while, hypnotized by his own thoughts.

"Come on," Crunch said and led the way off the pavement and across a one-way ramp to a stairway, then a maze of pedestrian paths. It took twenty minutes to escape the labyrinth of the airport and ten more to find the playground. Captain Crunch was so disoriented by then that he wasn't even sure it was the same playground he'd seen from the bus. It didn't matter. There were two hoops, a ball, and eight guys running up and down. They weren't very good. Most of them seemed to be either Hispanic or Slavic. No one said much. They mostly huffed and grunted and spat out dull monotone curses.

"These guys suck," Straughter said. "I can't play with them."

"You can play with anybody, kid. At least that's what your scouting report says. That's what makes you so great. You can take mediocre guys and make them look like NBA all-stars! Hell, I think I'll even play with you." Crunch turned toward the game and yelled: "Hey, we've got winners! Both of us!"

No one responded, but after one team reached fifteen points—on an off-balanced spastic hookshot—the losing four surrounded Crunch and Straughter, each guy hoping to be selected for one of the two other spots on their team.

Captain Crunch, ever the talent scout, made the selection: he chose a Puerto Rican kid with long arms and a Slavic kid who seemed to be the least tired. He told them both: "You are two lucky sons of bitches. You are about to be the teammates—for one fleeting game—of Jerome Straughter, the next Magic Johnson. You're gonna tell your grandchildren about this. This will probably be the most incredible experience of your lives...."

"Yo, cut the bullshit," hollered a shirtless member of the defending winners, "an' take out d'ball! Let's play, *pendejo*."

The Slav inbounded to the Puerto Rican, who drib-

61

bled up court. Crunch ran up behind them, alongside Straughter. "Pass Straughter the ball," Crunch hollered. "He's the point guard!"

The Puerto Rican eyed Crunch in dismay.

Crunch looked to his right. Straughter was no longer beside him. Crunch glanced over his shoulder and saw that his point guard had pulled up lame.

"Oh, my God." He ran over. "What is it?"

Straughter grimaced in agony.

"Talk to me."

One of the Slavs yelled, "Hey, old man, y'gonna play?"

"He's hurt," Crunch blurted in a frenzy, then added, "Give him some air," even though no one other than himself was within twenty feet.

# 4

# Head Case

"WHERE DOES IT HURT?" Crunch pleaded. "Please, tell me where it hurts!"

"My ankle. I felt something pop. I'll be all right by the time we get on the plane." Straughter was now limping gingerly as he and Crunch moved away from the court.

"Oh, God, what have I done?" Crunch's entire skin was a field of goose bumps that felt like staples. His eyelids bit down on his pupils, then snapped open quickly to see if this had really happened. It had. The young man's limp appeared to be serious. It was a reminder of Stan Hendrix, the Posse's 1982 center the night Stan was low-bridged on a breakaway by a UNLV forward, ending Stan's career.

"Relax," the kid said, his face still clenched in agony. "I'll be fine by the time we get there."

"That's what Stan Hendrix said. No, you are not fine. I am not fine. Nothing is fine. Everything stinks. I don't deserve the greatest offensive machine in the history of collegiate basketball. I don't deserve to have a point guard to run my offense. You should get a good lawyer and sue the crap out of me for dragging you out here onto this dangerous concrete. I should be shot."

"IS THIS A LIFE AND DEATH situation?" asked the 911 operator as Captain Crunch stood gaping into the cracked receiver of a nearby pay phone. Straughter was now prone on a park bench, his injured ankle propped over the back support.

"Yes, it's a matter of life and death." And he scanned the horizon for a street sign or other identifying landmark so as to convey their whereabouts.

Crunch's mental state deteriorated rapidly as he waited, splayed out on the bench next to his player, who became enraged at the sight of the approaching ambulance. "I told you I was gonna be all right. I just needed a few minutes. You're not my mother! I don't need a damn ambulance. I don't need a fuckin' hospital."

"I'll pay for it," Crunch mumbled through his catatonia.

"What about the NCAA?"

"We got a system worked out...."

The ambulance found them. The paramedics—a man and a woman—rushed over to Captain Crunch.

64

They eased him up by the shoulders and started to lay him on a stretcher.

"Hey, take your hands off me!"

"Did you call an ambulance?" asked the woman.

"Yeah, I called an ambulance, but...."

"Looks like coronary thrombosis," she told her partner. Then she asked Crunch: "Heavy pain in the center of the chest? Dizziness? Sweating?"

"Yeah, that's right, but the ambulance isn't for me. It's for him." Crunch indicated the young man next to him.

"You said this was life and death."

"Do you know who this is? This is my point guard. If he plays, my team lives. He doesn't play, my team dies."

Crunch rode along, crowding the guts of the ambulance, which seemed to be blowing its horn as much as it blared its siren, the man at the wheel cursing at drivers who would not surrender their positions on the road.

Crunch watched the lady paramedic brace the injured ankle and check the young man's skin for abrasions. Then she offered Straughter some pain killer.

"No," Straughter muttered through his agony. "I'll be all right...."

A good sign—that his threshold was high; he could play in pain—assuming he ever played again.

"Can't you do anything?" Crunch asked.

The woman shook her head. "We've phoned ahead to the on-call orthopedist. He'll meet you at the hospital. He'll take X-rays and assess the damage.... If it's any consolation, I don't think it's too serious."

It was a great consolation, but Captain Crunch did not let on. He just shook his head and muttered: "John Chaney could throw a hundred punches and he wouldn't be as big an asshole as me!"

The emergency entrance of Queens Mercy General was underground, at the end of a dark tunnel. Straughter was rushed through the automatic swinging doors and around a corner. Captain Crunch was shown to a stiff vinyl chair near a table piled with religious magazines.

He waited. His anxiety boiled. He harassed a nurse until she told him where the X-rays were being filmed, then he stood outside the thick wooden door and accosted everyone who entered or exited. He discovered that his point guard had to be sedated in order that he not move while each X-ray was shot.

Moments later, the unconscious Straughter was carried past Crunch and through another door. From there he was tucked into the bed of a semi-private room. Crunch sat quietly at the kid's bedside and prayed as best he knew how until the orthopedist, a languid man with furry eyebrows, peeked his head in: "Excuse me, are you his legal guardian?"

"I'm his coach. I'm responsible for the next four years of his life and for the molding and shaping of his character...."

"I would like to have a word with you outside."

Crunch got up slowly and lumbered into the hall, which had a sick cherry disinfectant smell. "What's the verdict?"

"There is nothing wrong with his ankle."

"What?"

"I checked the bone, the cartilage, the ligament. His ankle is fine."

"Then why is he carrying on?"

"I cannot answer that question," the orthopedist said. His rancid breath overpowered the disinfectant cherry aroma. His hair stood high upon his head like a fresh loaf of bread. He seemed to be shaking his own delicate hand. "If you want I can recommend a good psychiatrist."

"Don't say that! Oh, Christ, don't say that. Don't tell me my point guard is a fucking head case!" Life offered few tragedies more acute than a great basketball talent who, for whatever reason, was a head case. They not only were destined to bring themselves down—they'd drag down the rest of the team with them. "Please, say it isn't so. I didn't recruit the second coming of Mark Aguire or Ralph Sampson or Benoit Benjamin to run my team. Tell me, man, please!"

But the orthopedist just shrugged.

CRUNCH WANDERED the marble halls of this institution until he came to a large pane of glass overlooking the street. It was dark outside now and he could read the neon sign flashing: "MONA'S SPORTING GOODS."

He ran down a flight of stairs and outside. A cool breeze fought against him as he crossed the boulevard.

Mona's Sporting Goods was crowded with cardboard edifices of current sports heroes: Prime Time

Neon Deion, The Big Hurt, Shaq Attack. Boys of all ages milled about, trying on clearance-sale baseball gloves, gripping leather footballs, fondling footwear, and dreaming. Crunch could swear that he smelled the buttery exhaust of their little fantasy engines churning romantically inside their heads as they choked up on bats, hung catchers masks on their faces, aligned shoulder pads to their slender frames, and slamdunked basketballs on the official NBA rim and glass that was set up only six feet off the floor.

Captain Crunch leaned against a row of hockey sticks and stared in dismay, wondering how a young man for whom the superstardom dream was within reach could be such a colossal head case as to fake an injury. It made Crunch dizzy and a little pissed. The dream of roundball greatness is, after all, only as momentous as the dreamer makes it; when a head case expectorates on his big chance—with drugs or just mental inactivity—his spit lands on the very game of basketball.

But of course, there was another explanation for this bizarre behavior on the part of the kid; it was entirely possible that this young man was not a head case at all.

To that end, Captain Crunch bought a brand new Wilson leather official NBA basketball, signed by commissioner David Stern. The price horrified him. (The last time the coach had to go into a store and use his own money for a basketball Dave Bing was a member of the Detroit Pistons backcourt.)

Crunch dribbled the ball back across the street and into the hospital. He knew that it was not proper hospital comportment to dribble a basketball through the hallways where people are sick or dying, but he didn't care. Captain Crunch was a crusader of the great sport; he had a mission. He dribbled into Straughter's room and turned the lights on. Straughter was conscious. He was reading a newspaper with a grave look on his face.

"Yo, Straughter!" Crunch shouted.

The kid looked up and put his newspaper down.

Captain Crunch threw a chest pass.

The ball bounced off the young man's head and landed on a chair next to his adjustable bed.

Crunch retrieved the ball. He threw it again. This time the young man caught it. He caught it with both hands, clutching it to his chest like a sissy.

"You're not Jerome Straughter!" Crunch shouted.

He snatched the ball away from the kid and hurled it back at him. With a total lack of coordination and basketball instinct, the kid fumbled it against his stomach. A tear skated down his raggedy cheek.

"Who are you?" Crunch asked. "Who the hell are you?"

The kid didn't answer. He sat up in bed, held the ball over his head despondently, and, in an instantaneous fit of rage, hurled it at the room's dormant radiator, which made an unsatisfying tin rattle.

# 5

# *A Mind is a*
# *Terrible Thing to Waste*

CRUNCH AND THE IMPOSTER spent that night together in the hospital. Crunch got himself the other bed in the same room, explaining to the admissions clerk that he was experiencing an emotional break-down and might become a danger to society if he did not get a quiet night's sleep.

Captain Crunch did not get much sleep. He kept hearing the cries of people in traction, people in pain—and when that died down there was the cynical laughter of nurses. At 4:30 Crunch finally dozed into a heavy sleep, the kind that might have held up till noon or beyond if not for the hospital dietician waking him up at 6:00 with a tray of clammy scrambled eggs, a cold bagel, and corn flakes that looked as though they had freezer burn. Crunch looked over at the kid in the next bed and said: "Let's get the hell out of here."

He wasn't really sure why he said "we"—or why he even addressed the kid. Had Crunch returned to Four Corners with this sissy as his team leader, it very probably would have marked the beginning of his career as a junior-high-school PE instructor. He still felt a slight urge to strangle the kid, but he was not comfortable with the idea of just leaving him here. He felt obliged to return the young man to his mother and girlfriend.

Crunch reached over his head and pulled the telephone onto his chest. He called a car phone in Denver, Colorado, that belonged to a Four Corners alumnus named Kurt Crane. Kurt Crane was the COO of Mid-Atlantic Reliable Health Insurance Underwriters and also a very strong supporter of the Four Corners basketball program. His donations came in the form of vouchers for medical claims submitted by players who were not yet—but might soon be—members of the Posse. If, for example, the mother of a hot recruit needed a gallbladder operation, Kurt Crane would get a call. He could predate a policy back to the year 1960 if necessary. Crunch reached Crane and explained the situation. Within an hour, Captain Crunch and the young man who was not Jerome Straughter owed nothing to Queens Mercy Hospital and were free to go.

Outside on the street, the young man said, "Thanks for taking care of the bill."

"Don't mention it," Crunch said.

"Don't matter now, though, does it?"

"No, I guess it's not illegal for me to pay for your hospital bill—since you are definitely not going to be playing ball for the Four Corners Posse. But that doesn't mean I want the fucking newspapers printing a scoop about my little medical payment scheme!"

The kid slumped his shoulders, sunk his head, and walked across the street.

"Wait," Crunch hollered. "Wait up…. Who are you?"

"It doesn't matter who I am, does it? What matters is who I'm not."

"That's true, but who are you?"

"Dwayne," the young man said and turned and walked away.

"What do you mean 'Dwayne?' Dwayne who?"

Dwayne didn't answer. Crunch ran after him. The kid walked fast, and Crunch didn't catch up until the far corner in front of a barbershop that spewed opera music.

"Can I buy you some breakfast?"

"You tell me," Dwayne said, his hostility weakened by an obvious hunger.

Crunch felt the need for some Jewish food. Being in New York City gave him the urge to have some smoked fish swimming around in his stomach.

Dwayne was uncomfortable sitting in Haim's Deli. When their short, plump waitress rolled toward them with her pad flexed, Dwayne didn't know what to say, so Crunch ordered lox and fried matzo for both of them. When it arrived, Dwayne turned his plate so that the pink slices were as far away as possible, then he studied the fried matzo long and hard and cut it into small greasy crumbs. Crunch cleaned both plates and ordered Dwayne a corned beef sandwich to go. Crunch wasn't sure why he was being so nice to this kid who had set him back two days and hundreds—perhaps thousands—of dollars. Crunch reasoned that since Dwayne now knew of recruiting violations Crunch had committed, he'd better try to remain cordial.

They hopped a cab back to the airport to retrieve Dwayne's suitcase, then found a bus marked "Manhattan." Crunch paid for Dwayne and then followed him to a seat.

"You're coming home with me?" Dwayne asked.

"I want to know who you are."

"Is that right? You came all the way from the Arabian desert to find out who I am?"

"I came from the Arizona, New Mexico, Utah, and Colorado deserts—and you know why I came. And if you're as sharp as you seem to think you are, then you should have figured out by now that I'm not leaving the New York metropolitan area until I find the real Jerome Straughter—dead or alive. You almost cost me my job, kid. So I think I have the right to know who you are."

Dwayne nodded, as if about to say something, but never did. He hid his face within a ray of sun that bounced off the windows of the United terminal. Dwayne and Crunch were silent during the whole ride, which let them off on East 33rd Street, where they were accosted by a receiving line of beggars mumbling pleas about being lost, hungry, fired from the

Sanitation Department and the CIA.

Crunch passed out money for a while. He lost track of Dwayne and wound up giving *him* a dollar.

"I know my way home from here," Dwayne said, as they walked toward an uptown subway entrance, past people in suits and ties all in a trance against the onslaught of panhandlers. "Nice knowing you, man."

"Wait. Who are you?" Crunch demanded.

"I told you."

"Yeah, Dwayne. Dwayne what?"

"I don't owe you anything. You don't have the right to know who I am."

"Tell me anyway. Do me a favor. Be a good samaritan. Help a desperate man."

They were on the subway stairs now, climbing over a pile of rags that smelled like there was still a person in them.

"Quit following me."

"Tell me who you are."

"My name is Dwayne Straughter. Now, leave me alone!"

"You're Jerome's brother?"

"Leave me alone."

"Are you or are you not Jerome Straughter's brother?"

"I'm his cousin."

"You look just like him."

"Not really. Not if you saw us together. Jerome has a big head. I'm seven years older and much better looking."

"But you're cousins?"

"My mother and his mother are sisters, twin sisters, all right? He got the ugly genes."

"Yeah," Crunch said, "and the point guard genes."

"Yeah, I guess so."

"Where is he?"

"I don't know."

Dwayne hurried toward the token clerk and emptied his pockets, trying to raise the capital for a token. Crunch stepped ahead of him and bought two. "It's on me."

"I still don't know where Jerome is," Dwayne said, lurching through the turnstile and walking to the edge of the platform.

"Is he alive?"

Dwayne shrugged. "Yeah, I guess. Last time I saw him."

"When was that?"

"Couple weeks ago."

"Where was he living?"

"Same place."

"Same place as what?"

"Same place as me," the kid said, rubbing the bone of his narrow nose with two fingers. Again he leaned over the edge of the platform. Crunch leaned behind him and saw a light at the end of the tunnel, but he couldn't tell if it was the light of a train coming toward them or just a light that was always there, teasing those who had to wait.

"How did you know who I was?"

Dwayne shrugged. "I seen your picture. Jerome was showing it around."

"Why did he disappear?"

"That's his business."

"He didn't tell anybody where he was going?"

Dwayne shook his head.

"Did he ask you to pretend you were him?"

Dwayne shook his head again. His eyes had become icy, like he and Crunch were strangers—total strangers—and like Crunch was just some white man trying to make small talk. Crunch saw a pack of tough-looking guys smoking marijuana and blasting two enormous radios—one of them on wheels. Crunch reasoned that Dwayne was self-conscious about how they perceived him.

"So then it was entirely your idea to pretend you were him?"

Dwayne nodded. "My idea. There a problem?"

"No, no problem," Crunch said, intimidated by the threatening baritone now asserting itself from Dwayne's crookedly arched mouth. "Why'd you do it?"

"Do what?"

"Pretend you were him."

"To mess wit' your mind."

"I don't believe you."

Dwayne held the glazed hostility on his face for a while, then it faded. He looked at his shoes, then up at Captain Crunch. His eyes softened and got moist. "I want to go to college."

"What do you mean?"

"I want to learn. I want to get a degree…. Maybe go to med school…."

"So you impersonate a point guard and defraud the very institution of learning from which you want that education?"

77

"I don't have money for tuition."

"Get a scholarship like a normal minority student. Miller Light gives the United Negro College Fund a thousand dollars every time the networks show a game!"

"I had a scholarship—Towson State in Maryland—but the paperwork got fucked up; I got my classes but had no money for books or housing. I tried borrowing books and living in the park, but I got arrested for vagrancy, missed my midterms, lost my scholarship. Now nobody will touch me...."

"You gotta keep trying, that's all. Patience is a virtue, young man."

"Six fucking years."

*"What?"*

"Six fucking years, man. That's how long I been trying to get another college scholarship. The system, it's full of cracks, Captain Crunch. Some people live a whole life in one of those cracks."

"How old are you?" Crunch asked.

"Twenty-five, man."

Crunch bowed his head and turned away, looking for the light at the end of the tunnel. It wasn't getting any closer. He looked toward the indiscreet pack of joint-sucking outlaws. They were now raping a candy machine and tossing the Snickers and Chunkies and Almond Joys onto the tracks, daring each other to pick them up. Behind them, against the glossy tiles of the subway station wall was a mutilated poster advertising the United Negro College Fund. A young black man's sad face etched against the words: "A MIND IS A TERRIBLE THING TO WASTE."

"Did you really think it would work?" Crunch asked. He noticed, suddenly, that he'd forgotten about Jerome and the needs of the Posse, and he found himself unable to refocus himself on that problem, not as long as he was standing on this IRT platform with Dwayne and that mutilated poster. "Didn't it occur to you that you would eventually have to suit up and play basketball?"

"Yeah."

"Yeah what?"

"Yeah, it occurred to me. I was gonna get a broken leg or something…."

"Really? And how would you convince our team doctor and the X-ray camera that it was broken?"

"I'd break it. Really break it. I'd jump in front of a car."

Crunch shook his head. "You really are a fucking head case."

"I want an education, man. You said education was the most important thing."

"Don't twist my words!" Crunch was incensed. He closed his eyes on the kid and forced himself to consider the desperate plight of the Posse at that moment. Slowly, he began to imagine them. They were still in Port Huron, Sheriff trying desperately to achieve cohesion in time for their next tournament game, to find a way to set good picks for Jonny Never-miss-a-shot, to move the ball against a trapping defense.

But even as the coach thought about the plight of his team he had not completely exorcised his concern for the young man standing beside him, whose nervous perspiration floated up Crunch's nose like hot mustard. Dwayne Straughter was a head case, but Captain Crunch supposed that in the overall scheme there were good head cases and there were bad head cases, and that Dwayne was among the good ones.

What pissed Crunch off most about Dwayne's charade was that he'd gotten his hopes up so high, led to believe that Jerome was not only the greatest natural point guard ever to come off the streets of New York but that he was *literate*! Now Crunch was stricken with the odds of probability—that the real Jerome Straughter likely could not pass a sixth-grade English exam and that, if he ever did find him, Crunch would have to risk his job and his school's future by helping him cheat on the SAT exam.

Captain Crunch's eyes snapped open. He felt his hands come together and reach toward Dwayne's throat—but when they got there they did not strangle him. They held the back of his neck in an affectionate clutch. "You want to go to college?" he asked.

"I want to be a doctor," Dwayne answered.

"And Four Corners University meets with your satisfaction?"

"Man, I will kiss the ground of Four Corners University...."

"There ain't no ground. It's just sand."

"I will kiss the sand!"

A light emerged from the end of the tunnel—but it wasn't their train. It was an uptown express. A low rumble exploded into a great metallic roar. The train whizzed by the steel girders creating a strobe-like effect. The noise was incredible, but Crunch could not wait for it to pass. He shouted, the way a coach shouts

80

at his team in an unfriendly arena during crunchtime. He shouted: "Well, you can go to college, my man. You just help me find your cousin, and when we find him you take that SAT for him and pass the shit out of it…. I mean, don't do *too* good. A seven-fifty will do. You get a seven-fifty for Jerome and I'll get you into the Four Corners University—and you can be a doctor!"

# 6

## *Head Faking the Puddle*

HIGH MANGLED CHAIN LINK surrounded the Adam Clayton Powell Memorial Yard—a New York City standard issue playground—and fenced it off from the anarchy of the Harlem River Drive and the choppy gray waters of the Harlem River. The lumpy acre of colorless asphalt supported a small boarded-up building that said "rest rooms." A corroding sprinkler spat out a pathetic dribble of water, which no one showered in. (Across the highway, children danced in front of an open fire hydrant.) Two handball courts were graffiti canvases.

Crossing the highway overpass with Dwayne Straughter, Captain Crunch took it all in—seeing instantly, without surprise but still a sharp chill up his spine, that the only chunk of weather-beaten equipment being used for its intended purpose was the basketball courts.

There were two full courts next to two half courts. Six orange perforated backboards, all with rims, though two of them were bent downward—probably from overzealous slamdunkers. Each court held a whirlwind of lightning head-fakes, bullet passes, rainbow-arching jumpshots—an airshow of dunks, midflight fake dunks, a coast-to-coast, take-it-to-the-house, frenzied, twisting, leaping, derailed-but-still-zooming express train.

Surrounding the action a solid hedge of guys waiting for their turn to play. Some leaned on the chain link, glued by the electricity of the game. Others sat silently on the cement slab, scouting the competition. The only talking was on the court—"On his case...." "Mine, mine...." "Off left...." "Yo, I'm cuttin'...." "In yo face!" "Brick!" "Boo-day!" "Yo mama!" "Get that sorry-ass shit outta here!"—along with the snap, crackle, pop of colliding flesh and bone and cartilage. Up in the sky, dark clouds boxed out the sun. Captain Crunch could feel a slight drizzle spray the back of his neck. Other sandlot inhabitants, he noticed, also reacted to the rain, catching it on their hands and splashing their faces.

Captain Crunch and his new associate stood in the background. Crunch wagged his head in awe. "This is the way the game was meant to be played," he told Dwayne. He recalled a recent recruiting trip to L.A., to a court like this, only the backboards were painted white and palm trees surrounded the court. He'd seen

ten guys, ten strangers, give each other nicknames—
like "Red Shirt," "Beard," "Corn Roll," "Knee Brace,"
"No Neck," "Chipped Tooth"—then play with each
other in perfect innate sync.

"I just don't see enough of this kind of hoop,"
Crunch said now to Dwayne. "Sometimes I wonder
what the hell I'm even doing out there in the desert
with all that money and uniforms and play books. *This*
is real basketball. You walk out on the court. You
shake; you bake; you run; you gun; you operate; you
wheel and deal; you mix it up and let the chips fall.
No instant replay. No beer commercials. No cute-ass
color commentary. No inane interviews. Just gunners
against trees, whirlybirds against gravity, shirts
against skins!

"When you pay a man to do what he loves, you
think you're doing him the biggest favor in the world,
but you're not. You're giving him a big house and a
fancy car and making it so the world will happily kiss
his ass—but you know what else you're doing? You're
taking a wild horse—whose every poetic move is
improvisational—and breaking him into a house pet."

Dwayne gave the coach a once-over and gulped, as
if to digest it all. "Does that mean our deal is off?"
he asked.

"Huh?"

"Are you saying you no longer want to find my
cousin?"

"I didn't say that. I was just talkin'."

"Just talkin'...."

"That's right. Now I'm finished talking and I'm
looking around. I don't see your cousin. Do you?"

"I didn't say you'd find him here," Dwayne said. "I just said this was where he usually played."

"And you're sure this is the place?"

"I'm sure."

"I mean, let's face it, Dwayne, you don't exactly suffer from a basketball jones."

Dwayne rolled his eyes, then grabbed the coach by the arm and dragged him out onto the full court.

Crunch fought. "Hey, there's a game.... We can't go out there."

Expressing the same objective in a more direct way, the sidelines erupted:

"Yo, get the fuck off the court!"

"Hey, you ain't invisible, muh-fucka!"

Dwayne was unmoved. He dragged the coach all the way to the center of the court. Threats of injury and death assailed them from all sides.

"Look," Dwayne said, pointing at the cement.

Afraid to look anywhere else, Crunch peered down at where Dwayne was pointing. There were footprints and handprints stamped in the cement. There was a signature. Crunch made out a big J and a big S. The rest of the letters defined themselves in his head: "Jerome Straughter!"

"Those are his prints. He's a legend right here."

"Well he ain't here right now, punk," said a behemoth in a sweatshirt that looked like a potato sack. "So get the fuck off the court 'fore yo face be a print right next t'it."

"Yeah, come on," Crunch urged, still looking down, hoping his cooperation would win points with the angry crowd. He wanted to tell them how sorry he

86

felt, that he knew he'd committed a mortal sin, interrupting the flow of their game.

A giant hand raked his shoulder. It spun him around, then lifted his chin. A pair of green eyes glared at him. "I know you!"

Crunch beamed a terrified grin.

"You that coach. On TV. Four Corners. The Posse. The Lynch Mob. You a proper coach, man. You d'cream."

A wave of excited muttering welled up all around Captain Crunch.

The rake extended for a high-five. "My name is Kevin…, Kevin Crandel."

Warily, Crunch reached way up to high-five, then shook hands with Kevin Crandel.

"Crunch, that's your name. Captain Crunch…."

Crunch smiled. His eyes floated the immediate horizon. The angry mugs had melted into longing faces.

"I'm looking for Jerome Straughter. My point guard. Any of you see him?"

"Man, fuck Jerome Straughter," Kevin Crandel said, his green eyes palpitating, his nostrils flaring down at Crunch. "Straughter ain't shit. I burn d'muhfucka all d'time…. I run a clinic on his sorry ass…. He come down in the paint an' try to hang bricks but I's swat that shit, Federal Express to d'Bronx *Zoo* an' shit…. I got skills, brah! I cop him no slack on the inside, outside. The court is my office an' he my secretary, you dig?… He just a pretty boy, a cherry-picker coppin' cheap buckets—a pretender with a rep he ain't deserve!"

87

The rhythms of Crandel's speech had Crunch hypnotized. Crandel put his arm around Captain Crunch and walked him to the sideline. "Give d'man some room!" he barked at the other spectators, then to Crunch, nicely, "You just watch *me* ball…."

The game resumed, only it wasn't the same. The pace remained fast, the ball still whipped around, shots still filled the rim, but the poetry, the magic, it was gone. The ebb and flow lost its kinetic smoothness; it jerked with nervous vibrations. The aura of cool disintegrated from each player, leaving eight souls crying out like lonesome children: *Did you see that, coach? Did you see that shot? Did you see that pass? See that move?*

This was not the way basketball was meant to be played.

Crunch paid special attention to Kevin Crandel—whose recognition of the coach had surely saved Crunch from severe bodily harm. Crunch wanted genuinely to like Crandel, to maybe even recruit him for next year. Crandel had moves. He had quick hands, good footwork on defense, and a menacing karate scream as he snatched rebounds. Within the context of this sandlot game he shined, but he lacked the intangible—he didn't make the players around him better—and so his shine just was not brilliant enough to transcend the playground. Kevin Crandel belonged on the playground. Kevin Crandel would never make it in Division-One basketball. Nor would any of the other seven players on that court, all hotdogging it, yelling at one another for the ball, then hogging it up for the eyes of Captain Crunch—their ambassador of fame and fortune.

Crunch's eyes wandered—searching the sidelines for Dwayne. Crunch wanted to get the hell out of here but wasn't sure how he could gracefully depart. Dwayne was across the court, reading a stray page of an old *Amsterdam News*.

Rain fell harder. Crunch anticipated relief—until he saw that no one was leaving. The young men on the court kept playing; the young men on the sidelines kept waiting for their chance to try out for Captain Crunch and the Four Corners Posse. Puddles began to form on the court. They kept playing, splashing, sloshing, the ball slipping from their hands, sliding off the wet rims, dying on the wet ground.

One guy caught an outlet pass—on the money— from the other end of the court. He was all alone for a hoop. He spun around, right at a puddle. He head faked the puddle and went around it and leapt to jam the ball.

Kevin Crandel ran after him—*a la* Bill, the ever-present defender, Russell—in an attempt to block the shot. Crandel ran through the puddle and tried to jump. He lost a sneaker, lost his footing, and dove into the fence. He bounced off the chain link and slammed head first on the concrete. He sprang up and ran past Captain Crunch, his nose and mouth bleeding as he spoke with a macho lisp: "I plays hurt, man. I plays hurt. Don't make me no nevermind. I plays hurt. You think Jerome play hurt? Fuck no. He a pussy!"

Crunch nodded, eyes down, unable to face Kevin Crandel. Crunch wanted to shout. He wanted to climb to the top of the tallest housing project in Harlem and scream: *Who told you people that this was your way out? Who the hell told you the only way you could amount to anything was on a basketball court?*

But he was afraid he might get an answer.

Kevin Crandel's team won, and Kevin ran proudly toward Crunch. "I'm a winner. I does what it take to win the game, whatever that be. I got the winning attitude!"

"You've got a good game," Crunch said, cordially.

During the next game Captain Crunch did see a player who intrigued him. A guy with a tattooed head named Mel. Mel had no sneakers. He played in bedroom slippers and a sleeveless floor-length coat, yet he managed to outfoot everyone on the court and dribble the ball between his legs. His shot was unconventional—a kind of over-the-head heave—but it had radar.

Crunch, soaked as he was, began to see Mel as a potential point guard if Jerome Straughter never turned up. Mel dished well. He could slow and speed the tempo. Then Crunch noticed, during a trip up court, that Mel had a pair of tweezers in one hand. Mel's most miraculous bit of ball handling—also the one that ruled him out for a place on the Four Corners roster—occurred when, while toking a marijuana roach, Mel caught a bounce pass and threw an alley-oop to Kevin Crandel for a slamdunk.

On that play Crandel caught the ball above the rim for what could have been an easy jam, except that he tried to showboat it with a double pump and wound up fumbling the ball and smashing his head into the rim. He belly flopped into a huge puddle and rolled over, muttering weakly: "Foul, y'all. I was hacked. Kick yo ass, low-bridgin' motha-fucka! My ball!"

Soon the rain poured down in pencil-sized drops that splattered against one another in midair. Crunch could barely see ten feet in front of him. He reasoned, therefore, that no one on the court—still hamming it up—could see him. So he quietly stole away. Dwayne Straughter joined him on the street. They ran over the highway and found shelter inside Romeo's Bodega. They stood next to a barrel of white rice, catching their breath, the water dripping from their clothes and hair and making their shoes squeak.

Crunch sighed. "Forget it. I can't take this. I can't take another minute of this."

"Does that mean the deal's off?"

"Is that all you can think of? The deal?"

"Uh-huh. That's all I can think of," Dwayne said.

"I don't blame you. I don't fuckin' blame you one bit."

Crunch noticed the hostile glare of Romeo's owner, a stout man with a tomato skin discoloration across his cheek. Crunch moved through the store, filling a basket with canned vegetables and processed meat products. Dwayne Straughter followed. "So, coach, is the deal on or off?"

"I don't know, kid. I don't know. For right now, it's on, but I can't promise you anything. I may jump into one of these rivers before this is over."

Crunch paused before a gondola of tropical fruits. He had a craving for something very sour, something that would make his tongue bleed a little. He saw two fruits he could not identify and bit into one. It was sour. It twisted his face and made him shiver, but it didn't quite satisfy his craving.

Footsteps splashed through the front door. "Yo.... Yo.... Wait up...."

It sounded like Kevin Crandel.

Crunch grabbed Dwayne in desperation. "Is there a back exit?"

Dwayne shrugged. "I don't live here."

A body lurched past the dairy case. It wasn't Crandel. It was another kid from the court.

Crunch pleaded: "I'm sorry. I can't help you. I only have twelve spots on my team. *Twelve spots.* I can't rescue every kid from every American ghetto. I recruit all over the world. For crying out loud, learn a trade, young man! Finish high school!"

The young man ignored Crunch's obtuse rambling. "You said you was lookin' for Jerome."

"I guess I am," Crunch said, studying a transparent package of cheese that seemed to be wiggling with life.

Dwayne knew the other young man's name. "Earl," he said, "you know where Jerome is?"

"Not exactly. But I think I know where he at."

Crunch picked up the suspicious-looking cheese, tore the package, and had a bite. He thought he could feel unicellular life getting acquainted with his gums as the cheese slid down his throat, and the cheese was sour, but it wasn't sour enough. He needed something very sour, maybe even bitter. Something hard and metallic.

"Where? Where you think Jerome is?" Dwayne

asked.

"Place where Koreans come from," Earl said.

"*Korea*?" Crunch asked.

"Tha's right."

"What the hell would he be doing in Korea?"

Dwayne answered: "His girlfriend. Sunny…. When she had to go back to Korea, it had Jerome trippin' pretty hard. I think he even stopped playing ball for a while."

A thick nausea rose within Crunch's esophagus. Crunch gagged, recalling the photograph of Jerome and that Korean flame on the wall of Kim's Fashions. Crunch's central nervous system began to anticipate the bumpy sixteen-hour flight to Seoul, the truculent customs agents, the student riots, the unscrupulous cab drivers, the horror of trying to convey his needs to people through disjointed conversations over the opened pages of a translation dictionary. "Did Jerome *say* he was going to Korea?"

"I heard him talkin' last week," Earl said, tugging on his spongy wet goatee. "Couple weeks ago, sometime. Cryin' an shit. Talkin' 'bout a hair farm…."

"Did you say *hair* farm?"

"I'm hip…; an' talkin' 'bout a agent."

"An agent?" Crunch felt his arm stretched toward the beer cooler. It pulled the handle and grabbed a bottle marked "Luna Malt Liquor."

"A travel agent," Earl said.

"You sure? You sure it was a travel agent?"

"Uh-huh."

"Is that what he said? He said it was a travel agent?"

93

"No, he ain't said travel agent, but he said the agent was to help him hook up with his girlfriend…. Jerome was pretty strung out, bro. Told me basketball ain't shit when love puttin' them razor blades in yo stomach."

For some reason the image of a stomach full of razor blades made Crunch hungrier. He put the neck of the malt liquor bottle in his mouth and clamped his molars down on the cap, twisting it. The hydrogen gas within the bottle flexed its muscle, hurling the cap into the back of the coach's throat. Immediately, Crunch knew his craving was being appeased. He poured the foamy brew into his gullet, washing the corrugated metal object down until, with great pain, he swallowed.

# 7

# *Inspiration*

WET, THE SAD TREES around the Richard M. Nixon Housing Project seemed to come to life, shrugging off the rain with each sharp breeze. Children ran through the downpour, jumping from bench to bench, chain post to chain post. Two girls sailed a toy boat across a large puddle in the pavement. Two boys stood nearby using tail winds to aid them in a makeshift distance-spitting competition.

Captain Crunch and Dwayne jogged toward building number 3. Crunch's bag of groceries was coming apart at the bottom so that he had to bear hug the contents against his torso and chin as he ran. It was an exhausting workout; Crunch, who was always searching for newer and increasingly sadistic ways to condition his team, thought he might try it out on the Posse next time he got the chance.

Inside the lobby, Dwayne checked his mailbox.

"Any postcards from Korea?" Crunch asked.

"Huh?"

Before Crunch could repeat the question he'd already stolen a peek: all solicitations—one, an erroneous membership offer from the Northeast Millionaires Club.

"Mind if I leave you here?" Dwayne asked, offering Crunch the apartment key.

"Where are you going?"

"To work."

"You got a job?"

"I hope so. Public library."

"Go ahead," Crunch said. "I think I'll go lie down for the rest of the week."

But that was not possible. To Crunch's surprise he was greeted as he lurched through the front door by three crawling infants. He gently dropped the groceries on the warped formica dining table, and a pair of one-year-olds stumbled over and teethed on his Achilles' tendons; as he tried to get his bearings within the unfamiliar kitchen, a three-year-old ripped a box of Toasted Alien breakfast cereal from the coach's hand and ran off with it.

A moment later Crunch heard the faint voice of Patricia Straughter in the next room: "Clifford, where'd you get that box?"

"I want to eat them!" the kid shouted.

"Where'd you find it?"

"A man give it to me."

"Don't lie, Clifford. I'll whup you."

Next thing, the little boy dragged the lady to the kitchen; and then, as if she might not notice Crunch, the boy walked up to Crunch's right leg and laid his trembling index finger on it.

"It's all right," Crunch said. "He can have the cereal. I just need the phone inside...." A graphic on the face of the box had promised a lightweight modular telephone would accompany the sugarcoated glow-in-the-dark extraterrestrial-shaped corn puffs. Crunch knew he could not accomplish very much without telecommunications to the outside world and hoped it would be relatively painless trying to get the phone company to install a jack into which he might plug this cereal box phone.

"Where's Dwayne?" Patricia asked, wiping diaper cream off her hands and onto a stray dish towel. She was wearing a lemon housecoat and a lime scarf and stood gracefully, like a BYU player during the national anthem. Her marshmallow cheeks glistened with afternoon sunlight that snuck through the narrow kitchen window.

"He went to work. He said it'd be all right if I stay here. Is that all right with you?"

"Where's his suitcase?" Patricia asked suspiciously.

"We dropped it at his girlfriend's place."

"Weren't you supposed to go on an airplane?"

"Look, maybe I'd better get a room at a motel."

"I want to know why my son is no longer on his way to college?" she asked, pronouncing "college" with reverence.

"Things didn't work out," Crunch offered.

"My son is not going to college?"

"I didn't say that. He still has a shot."

"A shot? Don't sound good."

"A fair shot. Dwayne'll explain it to you when he gets home." Crunch was reluctant to confront this woman about her son's attempted deception. He felt an overall contriteness toward the lady—and was relieved that they were amid all of these soapy-smelling children rather than alone in the apartment. Captain Crunch did not trust himself alone with women. He was soft that way. Coming up in the coaching ranks he'd once landed a job with a junior college girls team and had to resign, unable to yell, to criticize, to make them run laps. He'd see a gal's eyes water and he'd say he was sorry. He didn't trust himself around too many women or around any one woman for too long.

"Would you happen to know where the nearest motel is?" Crunch asked, leaning toward the front door.

"The nearest motel is a crack house, mister," said the young lady with an infant slung over her shoulder and a toddler hugging her calf. "You're staying here."

"I don't want to put you out."

"I want to keep an eye on you while you mess with my son's future."

Proving to himself that his judgment was already askew, Crunch agreed. And, even before he and the young lady were alone—before the siblings, parents, and grandparents showed up to fetch the infants and

98

tots from this makeshift daycare—Captain Crunch was a rock turning to sand. He was afraid to swear in front of her—or even behind her—afraid to eat Toasted Aliens out of the box with his hand, afraid to belch or otherwise emit gas from his body. He was afraid to even *think* nasty.

It wasn't that Ms. Straughter looked at Crunch sideways or anything. For the most part, she politely ignored him. It was something about her manner—so sweet and unimposing—that made Captain Crunch feel like a big clumsy boor, made him want to be quiet, to hide in a corner somewhere. The scariest thing was he soon got used to it. He even kind of liked the way she silently put him in his place.

FOR THE NEXT FEW DAYS, Captain Crunch was content to conduct his search while relaxing in Patricia Straughter's housing project unit watching neighbors deposit their babies and toddlers each morning and then pick them up in the afternoon.

One such neighbor let Crunch use her phone in order to contact New York Bell and get a telephone connection at the Straughter residence in Crunch's name. Crunch plugged in the lightweight modular telephone receiver from his box of Toasted Alien cereal. He spread out on the sofa that was his bed and, with high-pitched whining and laughter of babies and the acrid smells engulfing his senses, he conducted his business.

Crunch didn't know how much Dwayne had told his mother about Crunch's mission—nor did he care to find out. A good coach thrives on the uncertainty of those around him. Crunch's first telephone call was to the office of Four Corners alumnus, former swing man of the Posse, Stu Grunwald, an executive with Divine Airlines in Columbus, Ohio.

"Stu, it's coach…."

"Crunch, I've been thinking about you…."

Crunch could barely make out what Stu was saying; it sounded like he was inside a washing machine. "How's life treating you?"

"I saw the Great Lakes tourney, coach. We're hurting for a point guard."

"No shit," Crunch said—and reflexively covered his mouth, clearing his throat. He glanced furtively at Patricia Straughter. She was preparing a bottle of watered-down apple juice for a baby whose laughter made tiny bubbles rise from his mouth and she didn't seem to notice Crunch's sudden lapse in civility—but Crunch still wished he hadn't said it. He wondered how long he could actually go without saying the "S" word or the "F" word or the "MF" compound word, if he really had to. He wondered if there was a treatment clinic to help him quit the habit or cut down—at least control himself in front of certain people in whose company he felt like an s-head—but then he supposed that, if there was a treatment center for the control of swearing, they probably trained you to use such sickening replacements as "sugar" and "fudge" and "I'm in deep yogurt!"—and that was too great a price to pay for civility—and anyway Crunch wasn't sure that players or referees paid much attention to coaches whose mouths did not bear a strong resemblance to a toilet.

"What can I do for you?" Stu asked, his voice all but swallowed up by a mighty roar.

"If I give you a name can you tell me if that name was on any flight to Korea in the last month?"

"What's the name?" Stu said and promised to have an answer within a week.

"Say, where are you anyway?" Crunch asked before signing off. "Sounds like you're in the cockpit of one of your own airplanes."

"Just about," Stu said. "This is a DC-10 flight simulator. I'm learning to fly."

"A jumbo jet?"

"Our union pilots are threatening to walk out—we're not going to let our airline go down like Eastern."

"Gotta hand it to you," Crunch said, recalling how badly Stu Grunwald had performed under pressure and then making a mental note not to fly Divine until their labor relations were restored.

Crunch anticipated his next telephone call to be a rather sordid one—one with which he would be unable to behave in a manner that children, or nice ladies who take care of children, should be subjected to. So he waited until 5:30, which was the time when Patricia left to take the last of her daily wards to the fortified garage where his uncle or cousin or someone worked. Then, fighting the urge to lock himself in a closet with a bottle of codeine-laced cough syrup, Crunch dialed the Four Corners area code and the number he knew so well.

"University...."

"This is Captain Crunch. Give me the athletic

101

department."

Sheriff answered. His voice was hoarse, his vowels quavered. "Did you find him, Crunch?"

"Not yet. I'm making headway, though. You think we can handle the creampuffs without him?" The creampuffs referred to the rest of the Four Corners preseason schedule; they played junior colleges and small universities—many of them without recruiting programs or scholarships. The Posse's margin of victory in these games averaged in excess of fifty points.

"I don't know," Sheriff said.

"Our first game is against Bean State."

"I'm not even sure we can beat a high-school team right now. Morale is low, Crunch. There's tension between the players. You can't let guys get humiliated on national TV and expect them to be optimistic!"

"Optimistic? We're not teaching a course on 'How to Pick up Girls' here. This is basketball! We need to get those kids angry!"

"I tried, Crunch. I told 'em my dead grandmother could play better than they did…."

"Gee," Crunch mused, "that hundred-year-old insult must have really got their dander up…."

"I did the best I could, coach."

"Lemme talk to 'em."

"Who?"

"The team. Assemble them at the Corral and hook up the phone to the PA."

"Now?"

"And make sure they listen."

"Can you hold on?"

He held on—twenty-seven dollars worth. He spent

102

most of that time inside his head. He tried to imagine what he would be eating for dinner. He enjoyed Patricia Straughter's cooking. It was heavy on the salt and made the ice water she served it with taste sweet. After a while, Crunch turned toward the window. The afternoon sun was a direct hit and highlighted all the smudges, but after a minute or so the sun hid behind building number 1 of the Nixon Project towers and Crunch could see the iron sky. He saw a pigeon hit by the bullet of a pellet gun and ripped from its flock. He flinched but kept his eyes trained on the window and saw, resting on the ledge, a row of green plant life. He blinked his eyes into focus and saw, through the dirty glass, a pair of strawberry buds.

"You there?" Sheriff's voice surged from the receiver.

"I'm here," Crunch said. "Are they ready?"

"Everyone's here except for Joe Mudd, who's in ligament therapy."

"Can you make a tape of what I say and play it for Joe?"

"You got it."

"Are we ready?"

"Just a second…. All right, hit it."

Crunch stood up and held the telephone vertically like a microphone. "Hi, boys, this is your coach speaking. I'm in Harlem, New York. You know where that is, don't you?" He walked to the window and looked straight down. He could see the desolate playground, the one without rims on its backboards. "Right now," he said, "I'm lookin' out of a window and seeing a ghetto basketball court. I'm seeing some pretty talented players. Dudes who'd give anything for the opportunity given to your pathetic asses. There's a guy down there name of Kevin Crandel who can fill it up pretty damn good. And he don't mind playing hurt. He's got the winning attitude. Hell, I'll bet I could assemble a team right here and now without having to travel more than three square miles from where I'm standing—so if you guys have changed your minds about being a member of the Posse, speak now...."

He waited. "Say Sheriff, did anybody speak up?" He waited.

Sheriff's voice stammered out of the speaker: "No, coach. Nobody said a word."

"Really?" Crunch said, feigning surprise. "So then am I to assume that they wish to play ball for us?"

"Yes," Sheriff said in a hollow voice.

"Don't speak for them, Sheriff. I want to hear them say it for themselves. Do you Girl Scouts want to play for the Four Corners Posse?"

What came out of the receiver sounded more like static than an enthusiastic basketball team.

"I can't *hear* you!" Crunch blasted.

The static got louder.

"That's more like it," Crunch hollered and nearly took a bite out of the plastic telephone receiver as he growled: "When you put on the uniform of the Four Corners Posse, you are not just draping your over-sexed bodies with pieces of rayon! You are adorning yourselves in the cloth of greatness. You are brandishing the colors of an institution with a great and proud history. A major university that sprang up—like some persistent vegetation—from the dry oblivion of

104

the desert to make it to network TV! A major university that has appeared in the NCAA tourney of sixty-four for the past fifteen years! Who made it to the final four twice! Which on one occasion made it to the NCAA championship game! And should have won that game—if it weren't for that scumbag, mother-fucking, shit-brained, blind, deaf and dumb Metro Conference referee, Hal Beckett, calling a loose ball foul on Lenny Hightower with time running out…. I mean, shit, you don't call fouls under the basket in that situation! Everyone is muscling and slapping for the ball. You let 'em play. You swallow your fucking whistle and let 'em play! You don't let the NCAA championship be decided on the charity stripe…!"

"Coach?" a voice projected from the receiver, but Crunch was in a trance, reliving that moment when ecstasy turned to agony. Four Corners had a one-point lead with five seconds left. Their defense was swarming. Kentucky put up a desperation heave. It hit the heel of the backboard and lofted into the air. Both teams crashed the boards and the pill was slapped off the plexiglass and out of bounds, just as the final buzzer sounded. The game was over. The Posse had run'n'gun'n'swooped'n'jived itself into basketball history.

Captain Crunch was sitting on the shoulders of his front court, tears streaming down his face, when he saw Hal Beckett waving his striped arms, gesticulating like a madman and blowing a whistle no one could hear. Beckett ran to the scorers' table and lifted the public address mike to his mouth. "Clear the court!" he ordered. "The game is not over. Foul on number twenty-two, red. Thirty-one, white team shoots one and one."

Crunch and his team ignored the intrusion unto their nirvana. They continued into the locker room and sprayed themselves with champagne and Raz Cola and waited for Brent Mussburger and his cameras to interview them while the president of the NCAA presented them with their trophy. But Brent and the president never showed up—and a closed-circuit TV built into the locker room wall informed them of the bizarre ending to a game they had just lost.

Kentucky forward Mookie Olsen's first free throw clanged the front of the rim, popped up in the air, bounced off the heel of the rim, then kissed the square, bounced off the front of the rim, then the back of the rim, then did the toilet seat twice—and fell through the net. Tie game. Bonus free throw: nothing but twine. Kentucky won the game.

Captain Crunch, writhing in horror, burst from the locker room and ran, dripping with ironic champagne, back onto the court. He saw Kentucky players clipping nylon off the rims, Kentucky cheerleaders tongue-kissing Kentucky reserves. He looked desperately for striped jerseys to protest to—this was the godforsaken 1972 Olympics all over again!—but found no one except Kentucky fans, Kentucky alumni, Kentucky coaches, and CBS cameramen—one of them now following Crunch around, the fat lens glaring at his every afflicted move. Crunch cursed at the camera with such venom and vulgarity that none of the tape could ever be fed onto their network broadcast (though friends of Crunch had since gotten hold of a copy and played it at the party following his four-hundredth career victory).

Crunch had searched the floor, then the officials' locker room and never found Hal Beckett—and since that disastrous evening, Captain Crunch had come to feel grateful that he had *not* found that incompetent zebra because he might have strangled him or gouged his eyes with the sharp edge of a ticket stub or in some other way tried to render the man incapacitated as a sports officiator; and since that night, Captain Crunch had made an effort to avoid Hal Beckett alto-gether—to forget the whole nightmare, to look ahead.

And that is what he did now to break the trance of this haunted memory.

"Team…. You still there, team?"

A static of acknowledgment vibrated the receiver.

"I'm glad we lost that game the other night," Crunch said. "I'm glad we got blown out by Bobby Knight and his all-American cornfed Hoosiers…. Let the writers make fun of us. Let Robert Montgomery Knight and Dean Smith and Nolan Richardson and Rick Pitino and Lute Olson and John Thompson and Denny Crumb and Billy Tubbs and everyone else write us off. Let the Columbia Broadcast System cut us out of their kiss-the-Neilson's-ass schedule. That's right where we want to be. Back in obscurity. Out of sight and pissed off about it! Boys, I'm gonna find your point guard and bring him back to Four Corners, and when I do, we're gonna come out of nowhere, like a four-on-two fastbreak off a made field goal, and shock the fucking world. We're gonna gush like crude oil out of the intestines of hell! You're winners—even if two-hundred million people think you suck right at the moment. You got something to prove. So let's look like it, talk like it, walk like it, and, for chrissakes, *play* like it!" And he slammed the phone back on its flimsy cradle.

THUNDER WOKE CAPTAIN Crunch the next morning. As he forced open his eyelids he saw Ms. Straughter, in a nightgown, performing calisthenics in front of the television. Seeing the knee bends and jumping jacks, Crunch had to fight off the instinctual coach's urge to holler: get those legs up, bend, stretch, come on, you chumps.

Instead, he told her, "Good morning."

The woman turned. Her body possessed a sexual bounce that had previously not been there. Or perhaps Crunch had failed to notice it. Perhaps he'd been too consumed with the Xs and Os of basketball to contemplate the Xs and Ys of nature. But he was still as consumed—perhaps further consumed—with his need for a point guard, and thus this lovely creature should have meant no more to him than that her twin sister's pelvis had pushed that point guard into the world, that their genetic codes had helped instill him with the gift of the no-look pass and the off-balance reverse layup. But, at least for the moment, as he sat up on the sofa that was his bed, sat in such a way as to conceal his morning erection, he found himself gaping at the creases on her sweatshorts and imagining.

The strangest thing was that he didn't feel at all self-conscious or shameful about this sudden sexual urge. The woman no longer made him feel like a

Neanderthal. In fact, her presence—the ease about tensing her muscles before him—made Crunch feel rather spry.

"Morning," she said back, and stared him over as if considering him in a new light. "What do you like for breakfast, baby?"

*Baby?*

"You don't have to fix anything," Crunch said. "I'll just have some Toasted Aliens."

The young lady returned to her workout until the show abruptly ended in a freeze frame of perspiring flesh. Then she turned it off.

Crunch picked his watch off a lamp table. It was eleven o'clock. "Where are all the kids?"

Ms. Straughter shrugged. "It's Saturday." Again she stared at Crunch, sizing him up, smiling. Was this the same shy young lady he'd seen taking care of other people's children all week? Another round of thunder shook the room. Rain rattled the windows. Lightning flickered. More thunder. Crunch's eyes began uncontrollably to eat her up. He began to wonder what it would feel like to chew on her mouth.

Crunch shook himself like a mad dog and tried to get perspective. He reminded himself of his primary purpose in life: to perfect the Posse offense. This thought, caught within the perversions now in his mind, made him wonder what kind of scion he and Ms. Straughter could produce—and how fast it could be incubated and grown and recruited into the Four Corners Posse backcourt. This was a very strange sensation for Captain Crunch who considered sex a biological function that Madison Avenue had turned into a religion. Crunch could only recall one act of sex that had lived up to all the hype. It was, in fact, his first time (long before he'd heard any of the hype), back on the farm in Oklahoma. He was fourteen. A neighbor girl, twenty-four, offered her naked body to him. At the time, Crunch had two acres of grass to mow and would not shuck his responsibility, not even when the girl offered a blowjob. Finally, the girl tied her naked body to the lawn mower and promised to keep her hands to herself while he performed his chore. She broke her promise, and young Crunch wound up mowing the same ten square feet for close to three hours. Since that afternoon, sex had, for Crunch, not even come close.

After two marriages and numerous girlfriends, whores, friends' wives, friends' daughters, and basketball groupies, Captain Crunch did not even believe sex was meaningful enough to compromise the skills of a basketball player. Where some coaches discouraged sexual activity for their team, afraid it dulled the edge, quashed the hunger necessary to win big games, Captain Crunch believed that the inevitable letdown of fornication would only make the player yearn for something more significant—like a ten-point, five-minute comeback climaxed with a buzzer-beating three-point Hail Mary.

But at the moment, Crunch's philosophy was threatened with revision. Perhaps it was that the lady seemed exotic to Crunch—or perhaps it was that she'd tortured his conscience all week and a rebellious part of him wanted to strike back. Crunch didn't know. He didn't want to know. He believed that he should leave

110

the premises before he did something he would always regret.

But before he could orchestrate a departure, he blurted: "You ever mow a lawn? I mean really mow a lawn?"

"Boy, *you* trippin'!"

"I didn't mean it," Crunch said, though he'd meant every syllable.

"Did you ask if I ever mowed a lawn?"

"Yeah, that's what I asked."

"Why would you want to know?"

Crunch shrugged. "It just shot out. I'm not thinkin' too straight."

"I vacuum the carpet now and then. Isn't that kin'a like mowin' the lawn?"

"Yeah," Crunch replied, biting his lip lustfully and glancing down at the carpet to see how dirty it was.

The telephone chirped in like a cold shower and engulfed Crunch in his coaching responsibilities. "Yeah?"

"It's Stu Grunwald, Divine Airlines." The background was quiet this time. "Crunch?"

"That's me."

"How are you?"

"Depends what you got to tell me."

"Well, I guess this is good news."

"What's that?"

"That name…, Jerome Straughter…. No such traveler to anywhere in or near the Far East. Not on any airline…."

"Yeah, I guess that is good news."

But then where the hell *was* he?

111

# 8

## *Bad Call*

THE ED KOCH ANNUAL United Nations Basketball
Tournament sold Madison Square Garden out. Captain
Crunch had to call Oliver Speares—former Four
Corners reserve, now a notorious New York ticket
scalper—in order to get a pair of courtside duckets
enabling him to convene with Bert Wafer—former
Four Corners starting backcourt, now a freelance NBA
scout.

"I'll bet you never sat this close to the court,"
Crunch said to Dwayne, navigating through an aisle
of folding chairs. "From here, you look *up* at the players. That's the way it should be. They are gods. We,
the coaches, the fans, the media, are mere insects."

Dwayne Straughter looked around. The rafters of

the garden shimmered with suspended trapeze plat-
forms and other circus hardware. Dwayne blinked,
dizzied.

"You see what your brother is missing out on?"

"He's my cousin."

"Yeah, right. You see what your cousin is missing
out on?"

Dwayne nodded his head at the layup lines, the
cheerleaders, the brightly colored banners.

"If Jerome signed with an NBA agent he's goddamn crazy.... Yeah, sure, he'll make his few hundred grand this year, but by next season he might be
in the CBA, playing for the Albany Patroons, riding
a bus to his next game in Montana. The NBA's a tough
league, kid. It's a what-have-you-done-for-me-lately
pressure cooker. You don't get many chances to prove
yourself. Guys who go hardship too soon can mess
up once and never make it back. I've seen it happen...."

"Where's this guy supposed to meet us?" Dwayne
asked.

"Bert'll be here. He's not scouting tonight's open-
er. He's interested in a Syracuse shooting guard and
an Estonian power forward. They play in the night-
capper."

"You tellin' me we could be home right now?"

"We could be anywhere right now, but there ain't
no better place to be tonight than at the Koch U.N.
Classic."

"We gotta sit through two games?"

"Gotta? Kid, this is the hottest ticket on the Eastern
Seaboard!"

"Don't call me kid."

Crunch threw a cocked eye at the kid, who twisted his mouth with apathy, then slid a paperback copy of Toni Morrison's *Beloved* out of his dungaree pocket.

"Just answer me this, Dwayne. Doesn't this excite you at all?"

"I'm here to help you find Jerome."

"I know, but...."

"That's why I'm here."

"Don't you care about sports?"

"No."

Again Crunch let his eyes roll up and down Dwayne. The kid wore a turtleneck sweater. But, of course, so did a great many collegiate cagers—preferring the turtleneck to the otherwise mandatory necktie when traveling to a road game. Yet, still, there was something about this kid—the way he folded his hands, the deliberate way he swiveled his head and measured his words—that made Crunch think, Yes, he *does* belong in a library or in a movie theater reading subtitles or on some panel of concerned speakers on public television or in medical school! But still....

"You don't even care who wins?"

"Why should I?"

"Why should anybody?" Crunch asked sardonically.

"I don't know. Why *should* anybody?"

"Because..., because those guys out there, they give their all!"

Dwayne shrugged. "So do I. Ain't nobody cares if I make it or not."

"It's teamwork, man. It's a brotherhood of man out there—a microcosm of humanity trying to beautify the world with some poetry in motion, some spontaneous invention, a do-or-die thrill-a-minute war where everyone—well, mostly everyone—shakes hands afterwards. Sure, you can be cynical. Tell me about how the players just want those big NBA dollars, the fast-food endorsements, the shoe contracts, their faces on a Timex. Tell me it's all a lousy business. Just another arm of the entertainment industry. You know what I say to that? I say screw that! It's true, but it's also true that we're all gonna be dead in a hundred years so screw it *anyway*.

"When ten guys get out there on the shiny lumber and that piece of inflated leather is tossed in the air, there's forty minutes on the ticker—forty minutes and ten time-outs and five personal fouls and who's gonna control the tempo of the game and who's got the thickest spinal fluid and that's the yin/yang right there.

"It's a lifetime of emotion compressed into two hours, and when it's over there's Gatorade in heaven and there's Gatorade in hell. And it's more than that, kid. Much more. If I tried to explain I'd be here till the next ice age. You should read about it, man. Put down them books about medicine and B-love and A-love and all that bullshit and pick up a copy of *SI* or *Sporting News* or *Basketball Weekly* and maybe you'll begin to realize that the United States of America depends on this sport! That every guy out there across this country—working a plow or driving a truck or working an assemblyline, and every woman poaching an egg or being a lawyer—needs to see Hakeem or

116

Barkley or Shaq or Alonzo or Karl the Mailman perform his job on the court to perfection and say, 'Yeah, I'm gonna do my job on the farm or on the highway or in the factory or the kitchen or the courthouse just like they do it on the hardwood.'

"Face it, kid, without the inspiration and example set by these giants of this game, the American economy would be towing a sinking barge—without the NCAA and the NBA we might as well be living in fuckin' Mexico!"

"Are you trying to imply that American productivity is reliant upon men in shiny underwear throwing the skin of a slaughtered animal through a metallic circle?"

"Look, Dwayne, were you picked on as a kid because of lack of coordination? Did you get teased and beat up? Why don't you put those bad experiences behind you?" Crunch said, curling his left arm around Dwayne's tense shoulder. "Hell, every kid gets his ass kicked at least once."

"My cuts and bruises have healed," Dwayne said, "but I will never bow my head to a bunch of greedy, self-centered, arrogant glandular freaks."

"You calling Shawn Kemp self-centered? A man who devotes hundreds of hours to helping the poor and the handicapped and the terminally ill to learn good sportsmanship and the game of basektball…?"

"Look, I got nothin' against Shawn Kemp or anyone else…."

"Then take back what you said."

Dwayne muttered in disgust and turned back to Toni Morrison.

"You think the guy who wrote that book isn't self-centered?"

"Toni Morrison is a woman!"

"And I'll bet she's every bit as arrogant as Wilt Chamberlain!"

"Maybe so," Dwayne said, his eyes flowing across the book's page, "but at least she has something to be arrogant about."

Crunch shook his head sadly. The sound of the Madison Square Garden horn sent its usual shiver up his spine—and yet to this kid it was just an abrasive honk.

"All right, Dwayne, you've made your point, and I understand what you're saying, but just do me a favor—do yourself a favor. Put all that bitterness behind you. Quit thinkin' so damn much and just enjoy the game. Basketball ain't something you sit there and analyze to death like baseball. It's a momentary bliss—it's like the drone bee that balls the queen and has one ejaculation and it's so tremendous that he literally explodes. So let this be the beginning of a long and happy relationship between you and the wonderful sport of roundball...."

But Dwayne remained uninterested, and the game that followed did nothing to change that. Puerto Rico and Vanderbilt played slowdown controlled-tempo offense and zone defense. Much of the game looked like a bunch of grown men playing "keep away." The buzz of the crowd soon became one massive yawn.

Captain Crunch waited until three hot dog vendors had come and gone before acknowledging his hunger—so that he had an excuse to evacuate his seat

118

for much of the second half as he waited in a long line at the snack bar, where he caught a contact high from the raging cigar smoke, which made his head feel as if it was a giant caster revolving around itself. By the time he returned to his second-row folding chair, Bert Wafer had arrived. Bert was now a bald man filling an extra large Hartford Whalers sweatshirt. His high cheekbones, puffed with corpulence, pushed his eyes into horizontal slashes. Crunch could not help but remember, for a brief instant, when Wafer was a wide-eyed, bushy-haired, scrawny guard on the 1976 Posse. Crunch wrapped his arms around Bert and they bear-hugged.

"Coach!"

"Wafer!"

Crunch introduced Wafer to Dwayne Straughter, handed them each a knockwurst on a bun, bit into the thick skin of his own bloated frankfurter, and then sat down to take care of business. "You got the names?" he asked Bert.

Wafer pulled a file from his attache and handed over a computerized printout. "I got every player with an agent in Metro New York, L.A., Chicago, and most of the boonies."

Crunch unfolded the long scroll and read. Straughter closed his book and leaned over to read along. The scroll listed every agent known to Bert Wafer and every player known to be signed with each agent. It also mentioned the league—NBA, CBA, or Canadian or European Leagues—and the team each player belonged to.

The first page produced no Jerome Straughter. Nor

did the second. The third, fourth, and fifth pages were full of penciled corrections, but no Jerome Straughter in graphite or ink. "How come all these names are changed?" Dwayne asked, finding more pencil marks on the sixth page.

"Big trade," Bert explained. "Just official this afternoon."

"Oh, yeah," Crunch said, "the big trade," not wanting Bert to know he'd had his basketball head in the sand.

"I shouldn't say big. I should say large, ponderous, but basically trivial."

"Low level," Crunch said.

"Very low level. You caught the whole thing?"

"Refresh my memory, Bert." Low level NBA trades always excited Crunch. Unimportant players swapping teams. There was always the remote possibility that these nobodies, starting fresh with another team, would click with the new chemistry and became solid players, even minor stars. "Tell me about it."

"Dallas traded Willie Pugh and a 1998 second-round draft pick to Milwaukee for the rights to Sherman Lark and future consideration, and in exchange for Milwaukee trading Hank Lapham to Atlanta so that Atlanta can trade Lapham to Phoenix for next year's second-round draft pick, which they in turn are trading to Chicago, who in exchange is sending the rights to Gus Anderson Jo...."

"Gus Anderson Jo?" Crunch flapped his head with bewilderment. "Isn't he an assistant coach now with some NAIA school in Florida?"

"Not according to this trade."

120

"Are we talking about the same Gus Anderson Jo who played the post at Marquette in the mid-seventies, then made the Spurs because of somebody's torn ligament and rode the pine for a while, then pretty much disappeared—except for a season here and there with the Wyoming Whachamacallits of the CBA or as a pansy for the Harlem Globetrotters or an occasional ten-day contract with a last-place NBA team in early April and an appearance at the Der Wienerschnitzel Summer League?"

"That's him. Been playing in Italy the last few years.... He's going to Jersey along with, get this, a third-round pick from seven years ago named Clauzell Thomas (who claims to have undergone arthroscopic surgery after tearing his knee up during training camp seven years ago when he wasn't expected to make the team anyway); they go to Jersey for future consideration. So go figure it out...."

"Clauzell Thomas?" Crunch mused. "Hey, I tried to recruit him when he was in high school. Somewhere in Connecticut. New Haven?"

"Small world," Wafer said.

"Sonuvabitch. Kid turned me down."

Wafer's mouth sprang open with sarcastic outrage. "You mean he turned down the great Captain Crunch?"

"Went to Georgetown. Said he wanted to be where the action is, said John Thompson is a genius...."

"I wouldn't argue with that assessment," Wafer said. "At least not to John Thompson's face."

"So the kid rides the pine four years under the genius. Serves him right, but I wish him well. I hope

121

Clauzell makes the NBA. I got no hard feelings. I hope the sonuvabitch becomes an all-star so every girlfriend he ever fucked can file paternity against him...."

The Garden shook momentarily as the Baltic All Stars stormed onto the court to mild cheers.

"You wanna hear the rest of this deal?" Wafer asked when the commotion had died down.

"There's more?" Crunch asked.

"You wanna hear it?"

"Not really," Crunch said.

"I don't blame you. It only gets increasingly inane. Rumor has it the whole thing was packaged by a New York agent name of Ray Meyers. He must have promised some kid on the Clippers or the Bullets that he'd get him traded to the Rockets or the Knicks sometime down the line...."

"Nobody likes to play for a loser," Crunch agreed, his eyes glued to the marked-up pages. He reached the end of the list empty-handed. He returned to the beginning and read it again. Dwayne also read it again.

"Jerome's not there," Dwayne said, finishing ahead of Crunch.

"Back to square one," Crunch said. He gulped the butt of his knockwurst and rose to get another one. This time he would have the concession girl spread nacho sauce and hot peppers on the dog. Maybe if he paid her an extra ten-spot she'd first boil the tube of meat in a pot of Schlitz Extra Dry. Crunch's mouth watered at the possibility, but he didn't make it out of his aisle. He was grabbed by a tall man in an ESPN blazer.

"Captain Crunch, Coach of the Four Corners Posse. I'm Barny Kobo, ESPN, isn't your team playing tonight?"

"No comment." Crunch could see out of the corner of his eye the lighted red dot that meant he was on live television.

"Would you like to confirm or deny the rumors that your son has signed a letter of intent to play for Dean Smith at Carolina—or respond as to the possible repercussions resulting from a failure to recruit your most accessible blue chipper?"

"Accessible? The kid won't even talk to me!"

"How is your team taking last week's blowout at the Great Lakes tourney?"

"I'd like to get a bite to eat, if you don't mind," Crunch answered, trying to force his way past in a gentle way.

"Just one more question."

"Please…."

"What are you going to do about your point guard dilemma?"

"I don't know! *I don't fucking know*! Do you know where he is?" Crunch asked, saliva flying out of his mouth and onto the interviewer's eyelash. Crunch faced the big video lens. "Do you know?" he asked the camera. "Does anyone out there in America know where Jerome Straughter is? He's a missing child. My missing child."

"And if you do find him, you don't think it's too late to pull your team together?"

"*What?*" Crunch almost slugged Barny Kobo, then

got control of himself. He had already behaved in a manner unbecoming a collegiate basketball coach. He smiled into the camera. "Hey, listen, let's not lose perspective here. This is not brain surgery or a cure for cancer we're talking about. It's a game. Sometimes you win, sometimes you lose. We're here to teach teamwork, sportsmanship, and the work ethic. If, in the process, you win a national championship, hey, it's icing on the cake...."

Unable to look America straight in the face, Crunch shifted his eyes away from the camera and onto the court. He saw the Baltic All Stars and the Syracuse Orangemen warming up. He saw the three officials huddled around at center court. He recognized one of the officials but, at first, remarkably, could not pinpoint from where; it seemed like he was an acquaintance from another life. Then the ref put his whistle in his mouth, as if to call a foul—and Crunch felt a scalding in his veins.

"Beckett! Hal Beckett!"

"So then would you say you were on a day-to-day with regard to your back court?" Barny Kobo asked.

"There he is!" Crunch roared.

"There who is?" Kobo asked. "Jerome Straughter? Are you saying you just found your point guard?" Kobo waved his hand toward his cameraman, trying to get an angle from Captain Crunch's point of view.

"Beckett," Crunch grumbled. "Hal Beckett. There he is...."

"Who?"

Suddenly, Crunch lost his sense of depth and everything in front of him felt two-dimensional. He reached his arms toward Hal Beckett and did not realize he was running toward the striped man, just that his hands were getting closer to the dreaded zebra's throat.

"Foul, my ass!" Crunch screamed. The words vomited from the back of his throat and felt toxic in his mouth like the return of last month's lunch. "Nobody had position! It was a desperation heave! It was a bad call. It was the worst damn call in the history of organized athletics!"

Beckett turned, suddenly hearing Crunch.

"You should have swallowed your whistle in those final seconds! You robbed me, Hal Beckett!"

"Easy now...." Beckett backed slowly toward the scorers' table and looked behind him for help.

Crunch caught Beckett by the throat. He grabbed Beckett's whistle. "Here, call a foul!" He shoved it between Beckett's lips. "Blow!" Beckett's eyes bulged out of his head. "So what if the game hasn't started yet. You know you like to blow your whistle and show everyone you're boss, and show everyone what a big prick you are! *Blow*!"

Beckett blew his whistle. Heads turned. The eyes were, to Crunch, dots on wallpaper. Beckett blew again. The dots grew bigger. Crunch reached out and whacked Beckett in the mouth, pushing the silver plated whistle through Beckett's lips. Beckett gagged, his face radiated a frightful shade of blue.

"Now blow your fucking whistle, you sonuvabitch! Go ahead, call a foul! Give me a 'T,' baby...."

Beckett, his eyes a pair of boils, drew his hands together perpendicularly, signaling a technical foul. At that moment, the other two referees, some coaching assistants, and some Madison Square Garden security converged on Captain Crunch, who felt his arms twisted behind his back, his head strangulated by a thick arm, his feet being dragged across the halfcourt circle of Madison Square Garden.

# 9

## *Ye Sons and Daughters of I Will Arise*

"WHAT DO WE DO with him?" asked George, the corpulent crowd control specialist, into his walkie-talkie. Crunch, in handcuffs, was alone now with George on a downward ramp somewhere in the bowels of Madison Square Garden. The ceiling was a rainbow of pipes, the floor aglow with layers of huge animal footprints.

"Have you called the cops?" asked an emphysemic voice on the other end of the radio.

"Jenks ain't sure we should."

"I ain't either."

"We can't stand here on ramp C all night," said Crunch's captor.

"How about security lockup?"

"No can do."

"Circus?"

"Affirm. There's a lion in there having cubs."

"I don't mind," Crunch said, full of remorse, trying to be cooperative. He craved the kind of emotional lift he might derive from witnessing the miracle of life.

"Negative, sir," George said, his eyes sagging toward his blubbery nose. "Lions don't dig no midwife shit. I let you in there she'll tear your face off. We ain't insured for that. You understand?"

"Fine," Crunch said calmly, hoping to charm George into an unconditional release. "Put me wherever you want."

George did. And as it turned out, the only room beneath the Garden that did not present a liability risk was janitorial station B-1, which, during the circus season, doubled as a storage facility for elephant waste. George turned a large bucket upside down and, holding his nose, told Crunch he could sit there. Crunch sat and held his nose, but the overwhelming stench still reached his sinuses. He tried to escape into slumber, only to dream that the smell was his aftershave and that he was lost in India, chased by a herd of elephants, who thought he was a tree.

Eventually, mercifully, Captain Crunch was awakened by George and a pair of mustached NYPD officers who carted him to their station and gave him immediate access to a pay phone. Crunch called Wilfred Glascoe, who'd once played power forward for the Posse and was now a criminal lawyer in Forest Hills, New York. Crunch reached Glascoe's answering service, then waited in a cell along with two car thieves disguised as Guardian Angels and a drunken man who ranted in Spanish with a Mississippi accent. The cell reeked of rusting metal and sour grapes. It was cold, and Captain Crunch's livid perspiration of a few hours ago began to solidify against his skin as he sat quietly and waited.

He waited all night. He wondered if Wilfred Glascoe was out of the country or dead from an overdose of valium or dead from representing too many drug-selling tycoons.

By midnight the cell was crowded with felonious zombies and a pair of confused Greek sailors whose uniforms were splattered with blood and Mace. The place developed a teeming dry-rot odor that intensified as the night wore on, but soon everyone was either asleep or spaced out, and the place was quiet; and Crunch could relax on the cold, wet cement floor and retreat into a trance.

"Hey, you're that Captain Crunch character," bellowed the morning guard, waking Crunch as he made his first rounds.

Crunch sprang to his feet. "That's me...." He looked around the guard's heft for a loyal Four Corners alumnus—and lawyer—but saw no one.

The guard maneuvered a powdered donut into his mouth, then offered its twin to Crunch.

"Thank you," Crunch said, reaching through the bars and keeping his hand outstretched, holding the donut outside the cell between bites so it would not be purged by any of his cell-mates.

"You make John Chaney and Bobby Knight look

like Mr. Cool and Mr. Calm."

"What do you mean?"

"Didn't you see the eleven o'clock news?"

"I was on the eleven o'clock news?"

"The ten o'clock news too. And the ESPN *Late Night Sports Wrap-up*. You was the lead story."

"The whole thing? They showed the whole thing on ESPN?"

"They said some of the tape had to be edited, but mostly they just bleeped the language."

"Shit."

"Yeah, like shit."

Crunch dropped his donut and collapsed against the bars.

The guard looked down at him. "Should I get a doctor?"

Crunch shook his head.

"Did you call your lawyer?"

Crunch nodded. He knew now why Wilfred Glascoe had not shown up yet. It seemed doubtful that anyone would make any moves to free Captain Crunch. Crunch had committed a first-degree blunder—a nationally televised violent outburst. Crunch had embarrassed not only himself but his team and the entire Four Corners University.

Put that together with their dismal outlook for the coming season and Crunch could anticipate the accomplishments of the last twenty-some years crumbling beneath him—network executives slashing the Posse off their regular season NCAA schedule, the NCAA tournament selection committee leaving them off the field of sixty-four teams. Crunch's son wouldn't be the only high-school blue-chip athlete to stay away from Four Corners. Alumni would grow apathetic—beginning with criminal lawyer Wilfred Glascoe who had better things to do than pull legal strings and spend political favors for a coach who had let his program slide and then turned into a psycho on national TV. There would be no more courtside Koch Classic duckets, no more preferential first-class tickets from Divine Airlines, no more inside information about agents. In short, Captain Crunch might as well retire—unless he could turn things around quickly.

And there was only one way to do that: find Jerome Straughter!

CAPTAIN CRUNCH SPENT the rest of the morning in that cell before he was released, with no explanation, by the police. (Probably a diehard Posse fan in the department.)

Crunch navigated his way by subway back to Harlem and discovered, as he mounted the stairs of the 125th Street subway station, that a strange thing had happened to his perspective. He was relieved to be back in Harlem. He felt safe.

For the first time, he noticed birds flying gracefully across the Harlem sky. He saw leaves changing on the scrawny trees. He spotted a flower—or at least it was a hell of a colorful weed—rising up through the surface of cinders and shattered glass. Crunch wanted to pluck that courageous piece of plant life and kiss it and inhale it and maybe press it inside a frame so he could always look at it. But he refrained, leaving it there in case some other troubled soul who passed by might get a boost.

Four blocks later, as he stepped through the Tricky Dick Plaza grounds, he fancied himself a soldier returning from war. He waved to a Puerto Rican kid sipping coconut soda through a dayglow straw, and the kid waved back.

"I'm home!" he announced, sailing through the threshold of the Straughter residence.

The telephone was chirping.

Fallout from last night's referee assault—Sheriff or some other concerned somebody from Four Corners wanting Crunch to make a public apology, throw himself at the smelly feet of the NCAA, or it was the media looking for a statement.

Crunch ignored the hideous chirp. He would continue to ignore it until Jerome Straughter was in his rightful place in the Posse backcourt.

"Sorry about the phone," Crunch said, finding Patricia mopping the kitchen floor.

"It don't bother me none."

"You sure?"

She nodded, plunged the sponge mop into an orange plastic bucket, made the sponge retract, spilling the foamy water, then squeaked it across the partially slashed linoleum floor. "Are you gonna answer it?"

"Not right now," Crunch said.

"It's been ringin' like that all morning."

"I'll rip it out of the wall if you'd like."

"I really don't mind. Just seems strange, that's all. To have a phone and not answer it."

"Huh?" Crunch could not concentrate on what she was saying. He was mesmerized by her mopping motion, by the steady thrusts of her hips as she fought the grime on her floor. He felt—or fancied that he could anyway—bodily warmth. It seemed to penetrate his calloused skin like a hot cup of tea poured into his soul.

"Are you all right, Mr. Crunch?"

No, he was not all right.

"There's aspirin in the bathroom. Maybe you'd better lie down."

"No." If he closed his eyes, his lecherous fantasies would run amuck. He needed to find something to do—an activity that would not only cool him off for the moment but for the next year or so. "Can I help?" he finally asked.

The young lady drew her head back and sloshed her mop around the pail, as if stirring a pot of soup. "You're pretty funny, Mr. Crunch...."

"I mean it," Crunch implored. He remembered how the act of cleaning house had transformed his ex-wife into a witch—how she'd accuse him of not loving her because he brought dirt into the house—and how his attempts to help her clean had resulted in a violent outbreak of flying ash trays, shattered Mr. Clean bottles, and general discord. Even after Crunch could afford to provide her with a maid, the romance never really quite returned to their marriage.

Now Crunch hoped that the act of cleaning a place together with a pretty young lady might once again transform his feelings of lust to feelings of disgust. "I've been stayin' here a couple weeks now, trackin' mud and soot...."

"You're here to help Dwayne get to college."

"I know, but I'd still feel better if you let me help you clean up."

"Do you do windows?" she joked.

Ten minutes later, Captain Crunch sat backward on the outside ledge, his legs tensed against the radiator, his butt hanging over the sidewalk. He sprayed Windex at the streaked glass. A gust of wind blew the Ammonia-D back in his face, stinging his eyes. He tried to get worked up about it—but soon the pain became bearable and Crunch could not evade the fact that it was his own stupidity that had stung him. He sprayed the chemical directly into the rag, then wiped, proud of his ingenious discovery.

After the windows were returned to their desired transparency, Captain Crunch opened a closet and found an ancient reconditioned carpet sweeper and pushed it up and back over the thin gray New York City Housing Department surplus shag. The handle, he soon noticed, was twisted, as though it had been melted and then hardened. Crunch supposed it had been a victim of the fire that had put the Straughter family out of their previous residence. The damaged grip intrigued Crunch as he pushed and pulled.

He saw Patricia dusting the coffee table, television stand, and other ledges and surfaces. Some of the dust caught onto her rag; some of it fell on the carpet, and Crunch was right there to sweep it up. Next thing he knew, Patricia was moving furniture out of the way for Crunch and his machine—and soon Crunch realized that his plan had backfired. Cleaning house together with this lady had created a feeling of familiarity that became a feeling of togetherness that became an overpowering lust.

Crunch tried to sublimate that feeling into his carpet cleaning. He made it an obsession, an unscratchable itch; the more carpet he'd covered the more be needed to roll on and on.

"Do you enjoy this?" Patricia asked, as she held out an empty plastic grocery bag while Crunch emptied the intestines of the carpet sweeper.

"No," Crunch said, truthfully.

"Do you want to stop?"

"No," Crunch said—also truthfully. "What's next?"

On the way down the back stairs with Patricia, carrying a heaping basket of dirty laundry, Crunch tried to reroute his train of thought. Though he'd asked several times before, he asked again: "Do you have any idea where your nephew is?"

"Either at the library or with that girl, Tiffany. She lives on a-hundred twenty-deuce."

"No, not Dwayne. I'm talking about Jerome."

"Jerome?" She shook her head. "He's a big boy. I hope he's all right."

"Yeah, me too. What about his mother—your sister? Where is she?"

"On vacation."

"Where?"

The young lady shrugged. "She don't tell me, I don't tell her."

The building's laundry room was dingy, windowless, dripping with graffiti, the machines vibrating sluggishly, weighed down by the massive conglomeration of locks suffocating their coin boxes.

Crunch helped Patricia sort out the whites from the colored clothes, then load a free washer. He noticed a twinkle in her eye and a coy smile. It had Crunch thinking that maybe she wanted him to make a move.

Crunch had forgotten what a little boy he was when it came to these matters. It had been so long since he'd had much of an interest in sex. He recalled a former player of his, a backup center named Harold Yolkem who, after being passed up in the NBA draft, got a graduate degree in psychology and studied at a psychoanalytic institute in Montana.

During Harold's apprenticeship as a Freudian analyst he visited Crunch and was aghast by his former coach's seeming apathy about sex. Yolkem explained that all human behavior and interactions were symbolic acts of sex. He had written a book examining the connection between the profound popularity of Mickey Mouse and the shape of his head and two ears which, Yolken contended, were surrogate breasts to children all over the world. Even basketball, Yolkem had said, to Crunch's dismay, was an act of sex: the rim a symbolic vagina, the ball a penis, the game itself a primitive ritual of men battling for dominance in the gene pool.

What did that say about being a coach? Crunch now wondered. What did that say about sitting on the sidelines, urging your team on?

Crunch was ready to overcome his inhibitions—but he also had his doubts. How could he be sure she really wanted him? Crunch was reminded of a TV show about the act of rape in which a psychologist said that many rapists honestly believe that their victim wants to have sex. Crunch had to wonder if he wasn't just a degenerate having hallucinations at this nice woman's expense? This was, after all, the same unassuming young lady who had, days ago, by her mere presence, made Captain Crunch second-guess his every word and gesture—had his perception of her mutated that much?

Crunch's mind felt heavy, soggy—until a minute later when it was flushed empty by the young lady's kiss. They were sitting together atop the washer, and Crunch couldn't even remember how they'd gotten there.

The kiss made Crunch feel young, experimental, and a little naughty.

When their lips parted, Patricia and Crunch laughed together and Crunch enjoyed a feeling of complete satisfaction. His lust was history. That single kiss affixed itself to his sense memory and, in the same way that a genetic imprint creates an organism from a single cell, it made his body feel that it had gone all the way and made love to her.

Only he was wrong. Minutes later, with their laundry spinning in the dryer, Crunch and Ms. Straughter were upstairs, doing things that compromised the security of the fasteners keeping their clothes on their bodies. And what followed was unlike anything Crunch could have imagined. He was a drone bee— dying and being reborn over and over.

"ARE YOU GOING TO FILE a civil suit?" Hal Beckett was asked by a faceless reporter at a live press conference over the local four o'clock news.

Captain Crunch sat on the edge of the plastic covered sofa, biting his nails, tasting the bitter residue of
Lemon Pledge. He'd turned on the television only
because he was afraid of what might happen if he and
Ms. Straughter engaged in a postcoital conversation.
He'd say something stupid and spoil the mood—like
he was now doing, out of control, hollering at Hal
Beckett on the battered Zenith: "Go ahead, take my
house, take my car, take my father's World War II
medals, take my Near West Athletic Conference
Championship trophies, take my Rotary Club Citation
of Lifetime Achievement…."

Beckett smiled at the cameras. His two front teeth
were chipped. He looked down at a yellow sheet of
paper and read: "Captain Crunch is a good coach and,
except for last night, he's been a credit to our game.
I forgive him for this aberration."

"Then you are taking no legal action?"

Beckett cogitated. "I asked the police to drop the
charges against him. I don't want to cause Mr. Crunch
any further embarrassment."

Crunch was outraged. His foot trembled, wanting
to kick the tube.

Beckett continued: "I just have one thing to say to
Captain Crunch—and to Bobby Knight and John
Chaney and John Thompson and all the other coaches in NCAA basketball. We refs, we're human beings.
We're not perfect. We make mistakes. It's a part of
the game. Throwing a tantrum ain't gonna change
that. So why don't you guys just give us a break once
in a while. You heard of National Secretaries Week.

138

Let's have National Referees Week...."

The reporters, their backs to the camera, broke into gales of laughter. Beckett had them in the palm of his slimy hand. The news returned to the sports desk. The ex-baseball player in a suit and tie nodded with admiration. "Quite a guy," he sighed.

Hal Beckett, the worst referee in the history of organized athletics, had become a martyr!

The telephone chirped. Crunch screamed at it: "You want a statement? I'll give you a statement! Fuck you! You want a martyr? You want a *real* martyr? Good, cause I'm gonna kill Hal Beckett. I'm gonna nail him to a basket stanchion!" Crunch got a grip on himself and didn't answer the chirping phone. "Not until I find Straughter. No comment until the Posse becomes the lynch mob it was always meant to be."

Ms. Straughter, who had politely left Crunch alone with his rage, returned, cuddling next to him with two cups of tea and a plate of baby strawberries she'd picked from the window sill. Crunch picked one up and admired it. It was the size of a grape but had the smell of a strawberry. He put it in his mouth and let it sit there for a moment. It stabbed his tongue. It seemed to have barbed wire in its skin. Perhaps it needed those sharp edges in order to grow up on a ledge in Harlem. Crunch bit slowly, warily, with his back teeth and broke the strawberry's hard skin. Its flavor splattered the inside of his mouth and knocked him backward, and then it wouldn't go away, even after he'd swallowed and sipped on some tea.

Crunch didn't mind. This ranked among his mouth's all-time great eating experiences—it was as

139

if a fig had been crossbred with a jalapeno pepper. Crunch wished it could stay there between his gums forever, so he could somehow preserve the romance of this lazy afternoon, but that didn't happen: the sun set, the hot berry taste disintegrated, and the complexities of life caught up.

"I suppose we shouldn't tell Dwayne about this," Crunch suggested.

"About what?" Ms. Straughter said.

"Yeah, right."

CRUNCH DID NOT WAIT for Dwayne to come home. He kissed the young lady goodbye and ran to the Duke Ellington branch of the New York Public Library. He stood in the oak-paneled periodical section, next to a window with heavy iron bars on the outside, waiting for Dwayne to clock out. Crunch tried to ignore the local newspapers and their sports sections but was overcome with masochistic curiosity. He picked up the *Post*, found the sports page, saw the headline:

### CRUNCH GOES SOGGY AT GARDEN

Crunch chuckled—a coach has got to be able to laugh at himself—until he saw the subheading:

### Coach Punches Ref
### *Meanwhile Posse*
### *Surrenders to Bean State*

"Coach," Dwayne whispered on his way to the

front door.

"Don't be so sure," Crunch whispered back, following.

"I thought you were in jail."

"I was."

"That guy you attacked, I heard he's in a coma."

No, Crunch shook his head. "Beckett doesn't lose consciousness until the last two minutes of a game."

"Why'd you hit him?"

"Because he made the most ridiculous call in the history of collegiate athletics!"

"I don't understand...."

"He disgraced the game of basketball and cost my team the NCAA crown!"

"Isn't college athletics supposed to be about sportsmanship?"

"Not as long as they hire blind men to officiate. I mean, is there anything worse than an idiot in a uniform screwin' up your life? How would you feel if a cop busted you for a crime you didn't commit."

"It happened a couple months ago—over on 112th Street. I got picked up for lighting a base-head on fire."

"Didn't you want to take that cop and crack his skull and watch it drip?"

"No, I didn't. I just wanted to get home. I wanted to forget it happened. Revenge is a boomerang, Captain Crunch. It's not the way to get over in this mind-your-own-business world."

"Who said anything about revenge? I'm talking about standing up to unfairness."

"That's a luxury around here, man."

141

Crunch was unhinged. He knew the kid was right!

Dwayne was sharply dressed in khaki slacks, with a seasoned leather jacket and a tie that resembled a sliver of beef jerky. He had a pile of books under one arm, and Crunch imagined the kid was hungry to get home and read those books. But when he considered Dwayne's animate face, it lacked the hunger. It seemed resigned behind a pair of round spectacles, resigned to the Dewey decimal system. This was something that always frightened Crunch—to see a kid (or anyone) lose that hunger, that itch.

"Got any ideas where Jerome might be?" Crunch asked.

"Na, man. You wanna hit the rest of the playgrounds?"

"When did you become Mr. Basketball Geography?"

"Fetchin' Jerome's little behind when he was late for dinner."

"Well, this time his little behind's about two months late for dinner."

Dwayne showed Crunch all the major playgrounds in West Harlem and some in East Harlem. It was an eerie tour. Under the black sky, Harlem lost its charm and gave way to a heightened desperation. Packs of men and packs of boys clung to street corners—as if the illumination of a lamppost defined their existence. Other people leaned on fire escapes or out of windows, staring at the darkness. Music blared on portable boom boxes, too loud to enjoy and in some cases off key for want of new batteries.

For the first time since arriving in Harlem, Captain

Crunch found himself afraid, really concerned about his safety. But Dwayne seemed to know all of the most nefarious-looking dudes—at least enough to exchange a nod and a "What's-up?" And the only people to accost them were a pair of drunken Puerto Rican men who recognized Crunch and asked him to autograph the photo of him attacking Hal Beckett which appeared in the sports section of their *El Diario*, above the caption: "*Capitan Crunch se a vuelto loco!*"

There was no sign of Jerome Straughter anywhere—on or off the asphalt. Dwayne and Crunch even swung by a strip of the Harlem River Drive where Jerome had enjoyed watching the moonlight with his girlfriend before she had returned to Korea. No Jerome. Nor were there any clues as to his present whereabouts other than one dead-end claim that Jerome was now working as a bouncer at a dance club called "Said So."

Nor was there any fanfare for Captain Crunch—no showboating, no tryouts for the Posse. The soggy Captain Crunch was no longer anybody's ticket out of the ghetto. For all Crunch knew, he had already been fired.

When it started to rain, and when gusty winds made even layups an aerodynamic uncertainty, the games abruptly ended, the players fled the courts.

"Where to now?" Crunch asked, sitting alone with Dwayne in the shelter of a stripped Buick Regal in a gutted lot adjacent to the IS 88 playground.

"Church," Dwayne said.

"No shit," Crunch agreed. What else was there left to do but pray?

But that wasn't what Dwayne had in mind. "This is where Jerome and his partners play when the weather's inclement," Dwayne said as they entered the gym of the Harlem Baptist Church. Jerome, however, was not among the sweating black men on the creaky wooden floor pounding the blackened leather ball.

Dwayne and Crunch moved on. They took an ecumenical tour of Harlem and saw some very impressive talent, but no one like Jerome—no one who could transform the Posse from a school of guppies to collegiate piranhas. The young players were all great athletes, but the really great *players* were the older guys. Guys in their thirties, forties, even fifties—with unorthodox jumpshots that filled up the hoops, with cagey moves and swift (if a bit arthritic) hands. Guys who'd missed the boat when they were twenty or never had a ticket, or maybe never wanted a ticket—at least not badly enough.

Crunch found the same story at churches throughout the Bronx and in various sections of Brooklyn, until, at nearly midnight, as they approached the Ye Sons and Daughters of I Will Arise parish on East Conduit Avenue in Bedford-Stuyvesant, Crunch was on the verge of prayer, of throwing himself on the mercy of the Lord, whichever lord could be contacted in the confines of this particular house of worship.

Ye Sons and Daughters of I Will Arise church was comprised of a row of converted storefronts. Above the main entrance, a crucifix was artfully painted over a gargoyle the shape of a shoe. The outside of the gymnasium still wore the "Fluff'n'fold" sign from its days as a laundromat. The gym's front door was shattered glass. Behind it, an old king-sized mattress. Behind it, those familiar clops and bounces and grunts of a basketball game.

Crunch was reluctant to enter, but the rain fell in sheets now, so he grabbed the handle beside the shattered glass and pulled. As Crunch opened the door, a young man in cutoff sweats and a gold headband came flying out onto the street, chasing a loose ball to the white line, then hurling it back through the door. The kid jogged back inside. Crunch and Dwayne followed. The moment they stepped through the doorway, they were on the basketball court, at the baseline. There were no seats. There was no out of bounds, only four walls—three of cracked plaster, one of mattresses shielding broken glass—and a fifteen-foot ceiling that obstructed high-arching shots. It was as if someone had invented a new game, a hybrid of racquetball and hoops.

Crunch and Dwayne tried to stay out of the way of the game, but that was impossible: the ball kept whizzing at them; players used them as picks to cut off of and take shots behind. Crunch kept expecting someone to jump in their faces and tell them to get the hell out, but no one did. Perhaps it was customary for people to wander through the court like this in the middle of a furious game; or perhaps they were just being hospitable because the gym was part of a church.

The latter theory was supported when one of the players, while cutting baseline, handed Crunch and Dwayne each a piece of paper that welcomed them to the congregation and invited them to Saturday night and Sunday morning services, a Tuesday and Thursday night bible discussion group, and a Friday night dance and raffle. A moment later, when a rebound was slammed into Crunch's stomach, that same Mr. Welcome genuflected before snatching the ball from beneath Crunch's collapsing knees. Crunch keeled over and was whacked in the head by the elbows of two players muscling for low box position.

"You all right?" Dwayne asked, helping Crunch to his feet.

"Let's get out of here," Crunch wheezed, leaning heavily on Dwayne's arm. "I don't see Jerome, do you?"

Dwayne carried Crunch to the door and reached behind the mattress, gingerly trying to grab the handle without cutting his hand on any broken glass. As he got the door open, he had to tilt Crunch's limp body around the edge. In doing so, Crunch's face was pointed back at the game. He flinched, half expecting the ball to zoom toward his helpless head, but it did not. Instead he saw a blurry and familiar face inches from his own. The eyes of this familiar face looking up, trying to gauge the hop of a rebound.

The face was darn familiar. So familiar Crunch took it for a mirage. True, he was in Brooklyn, but he was also semiconscious. He kept looking until his bleariness subsided and the face clarified.

It was real.

It was the first legitimate clue Captain Crunch had as to the whereabouts of Jerome Straughter.

But he had to be sure.

"Wait, not yet," Crunch said to Dwayne, who had

started to drag him through the doorway.

Dwayne froze. Crunch waited for play to return to this end of the court, then waited for the precise moment. It would have to be a pause, a made basket, so that the face could hear and turn around and confirm Crunch's suspicions.

Crunch kept track of the face. He noticed the body that the face belonged to. It had become fat. Each knee wore a severe brace, but the hands remained quick, the footing still graceful, if a bit lethargic. It took three trips down the court and two accidental elbows to Captain Crunch's chest before a ball swished the nylon. Crunch watched the familiar face. It smiled; it was, after all, his shot that had just filled the basket. The guy turned, running to the other end of the floor to play defense.

"Hey, Clauzell…! Clauzell Thomas!"

He turned. "Yeah, what?"

"It's you."

The guy frowned, startled, outraged. "No, man, it ain't. Bullshit, man. Fuck you. I thought you asked if I was from the Bahamas…."

"You're from New Haven, Connecticut, Clauzell, and I may not be a genius like John Thompson, but I ain't no fool either," Crunch said, and then stumbled out onto the street without any help.

"What was that all about?" Dwayne asked. The rain had slowed to a drizzle, though the street was still partly underwater and the two men had to walk next to the building walls to avoid the splashes from passing cars and buses.

"Remember that trade? That big NBA trade Bert

147

Wafer told us about?"

No, Dwayne shook his head.

"Well, I'll refresh your memory. Part of the deal sent a guy named Clauzell Thomas to the New Jersey Nets."

"Yeah, all right; I remember," Dwayne shrugged. "What's it mean?"

"What's it *mean*?" Crunch bellowed, as they passed a giant garbage dumpster, half covered, in which a dozen cats and three homeless men sought shelter from—and obviously did not trust the lull in—the downpour. "If Clauzell is with the Nets, then how come I saw him just now in that church?"

"Maybe there are two guys named Clauzell Thomas," Dwayne suggested.

"You're goddamn right there are," Crunch said, licking his chops. "And I got a very strong feeling one of them is your cousin, Jerome...."

# 10

## *Pimps*

"MEYERS AGENCY, PLEASE HOLD...."

Crunch held. He was prepared to hold all morning and afternoon and evening and all month—and watch the shadows on these apartment walls rise and bend, expand and shrink. He had his dander up. The plastic sofa cover beneath him steamed up from the sheer heat of his mood.

"Yes," the voice of a young man came back on the line. It was one of those trained voices that seems to have hydraulics behind it. "How may I help you?"

"I need to speak to Mr. Meyers."

"Who, may I ask, is calling?"

"Who's calling? I'll tell you who's calling. Coach Nick Cruschenctuwitz from Four Corners University.... Captain Crunch!" Crunch braced himself, anticipating the click and dial tone of a hangup.

"How's eleven this morning?" asked the young man.

"Beg your pardon?"

"Or anytime after two-thirty this afternoon if that's more convenient.... Mr. Meyers is anxious to meet you...."

"He is?" Crunch was puzzled. He felt his outrage begin to slip and tried to boost it back. "I mean, yeah, he'd better be anxious to see me.... I got the goods on his ass!"

As he hung up the telephone, Crunch saw Dwayne sail past him and grab the handle of the front door.

"Where you goin'?"

"To work."

"Didn't you catch my end of that powwow?"

"I was brushing my teeth."

"Well, good, because we've got a bargaining session with a certain kidnapping agent in about an hour."

Dwayne did not seem excited.

"Don't worry about the job, son. You'll be at Four Corners attending classes before the week is out."

Dwayne nodded and smiled, but his eyes hung heavily and his pallor seemed parched.

"Hey, I don't blame you, kid. I'm gonna be kinda sad to leave here myself."

"Do I have to go with you this morning?"

"Hell no, you don't."

"I'm supposed to meet Tiffany for lunch."

"No problem. I think I can find this Avenue of the Americas locale on my own. Just didn't want you to think I'd benched you or anything. The deal's still on, son. I'm a man of my word."

Dwayne arched his eyebrows and nodded. "You mean well," he said.

"What's that supposed to mean?" Crunch asked, but Dwayne had slipped out through the door and was gone.

On his way to the 125th Street subway station, Captain Crunch stopped at Kim's Fashions and bought himself a double-breasted suit so that he would blend in when he got downtown and suggest a fraternal appearance even though his objective was to kick some ass.

Crunch looked forward to a speedy ride—a forty-five-mile-per-hour straight line that would help him maintain his mental and emotional blinders and hold onto that hostile energy he'd had earlier on the phone. But as the IRT express train roared through the tunnel, the lights flickering clumsily, the other passengers frozen in a collective trance of newspapers, paperbacks, and slumber, Crunch's mind lost its sharp focus. He wondered about Dwayne's sudden listlessness.

Was the kid afraid of having his dream fulfilled?

Crunch had heard of people suffering such lapses of sanity—afraid of not knowing what to do at the top of the mountain—though he could never comprehend why, given the fact that John Wooden had won the NCAA title seven years in a row!

Between the 96th and 72nd Street IRT express stations, an altercation broke out in Crunch's car, which further disrupted his singular objective.

151

The riff involved a man in tight pants and two young women in wigs. Much of the heated exchange was, to Crunch, unintelligible, but he did think he heard the man refer to the two girls as "bitches," "sluts," and "smelly fuckin' coin slots" and promise to kill them if he ever found out they were working for someone else.

"You gonna spend us, huh?" One of the girls scoffed. She wore a purple body-stocking and a skirt that appeared to have been woven out of the skins of rodents. From beneath the skirt, she pulled a hunting knife and waved it at the man's face.

The man backed into a corner, his eyes hypnotized by the corrugated blade. "This family, baby. I'm yo bitch, you *my* bitch...." Then he kicked her in the chest.

The other girl whipped an antique hatpin out of her hot pants and stabbed the insincere man while her friend caught her breath and together they attacked their pimp, cutting his leather jacket, shredding his nylon shirt, and slicing his chest.

A number of passengers quietly fled the car. Others stood up and cheered the two girls on. Crunch sat still, gaping with astonishment. He was, in fact, the only person in the whole car still in his seat, and when the two girls were finished mutilating the torso of their former employer, it was Crunch's lap into which he was deposited.

Later, at the 42nd Street station, concerned about his outward appearance—and hoping to remove the bloodstains from his suit coat—Crunch found a men's room. He held his nose against the putrid odor. He saw a mirror enshrouded with a cobweb of graffiti, but Crunch might still have been able to find a large enough patch of reflection to at least fix his hair had his attention not been riveted to the pile of neglected humanity lying beneath a dingy sink.

Crunch could not tell if it was a man or a woman or if it was alive or dead. Hair was overgrown and brittle and splayed across his or her back, and beneath one arm a beehive hung, as if from a tree limb. Seeing this, Crunch could not imagine that it mattered what his own suit and hair looked like.

Later, however, inside the climate controlled lobby of 112 Avenue of the Americas, waiting for the elevator that stopped only at floors thirty through forty-five, Crunch worried again about the impression he would make with the young man who answered the phones for Ray Meyers.

The young man's name, it turned out, was Stewart. He reminded Crunch of a button-nosed blackjack dealer he'd once lost seven hundred dollars to in Reno. "Mr. Meyers is waiting for you," Stewart said, without looking up at Crunch's hair or down at the blood-stained shoulders. "Would you like a drink?"

"Water'll be fine"

"What kind?"

"Excuse me?"

"We have Evian, Calistoga, Beaumont, Stengal, Perrier, and Duckwell…."

Crunch, at a loss, said, "I'll have a little of each."

The young man showed Crunch into a large office. Hardwood floors made the captain's shoes tap as he approached an empty wing chair next to a glistening aluminum desk piled with debris. At the moment, there was no one on the other side of the table, but Crunch heard the rumblings of a sink and the slurp of soap and water, and he supposed Mr. Meyers was washing his hands in a private bathroom.

"I'm sorry about the way I look," Crunch said, as Mr. Meyers emerged from behind a door.

Meyers broke into a smile, his richly tanned face breaking a ripple of round wrinkles, like a pond catching a stone, his eyes shrinking, his brows lifting as if to suspend this moment of mirth.

Crunch was relieved by this reaction but also a bit confused.

"You look perfect," Meyers said. "Just perfect."

*You gonna barbecue me for lunch?* Crunch thought.

Stewart entered with a platter of bottled waters and two glasses—one with ice, one without. Crunch grabbed a plastic bottle with a label that resembled a Sierra Club pamphlet. He twisted off the lid, which had a cork in it. He wasn't sure if he was supposed to sniff it before he poured.

"I've been fielding calls for you all morning," Meyers told Crunch. "I hope you don't mind. I know we don't have an agreement yet, but.... Say, you're not talking to any other agents at present are you?"

"No," Crunch said, bewildered. "Why should I be?"

The telephone rang, then an intercom buzzed. Meyers apologized for the interruption, answering the phone. It was a client, a hockey player. Something about fighting and suspension without pay last season and suing the NHL office. That exchange was cut short by a call from "Delfo Zubiati and his transla-

154

tor" about a possible opportunity as a place kicker with the Tampa Bay Bucks.

At first these little inside tidbits of information were tantalizing to Crunch and he listened attentively— imagining all the conversational mileage he'd get back at Four Corners out of this exclusive gossip—but after a while, the endless names of sports executives and the tedium of Mr. Meyers's verbal ego-massaging, caused Crunch to lose interest.

He distracted himself by looking around at all the photographs of Meyers and his clients, seeing which baseball, football, basketball, hockey, and tennis players he could recognize. He noticed, on a marble mantle (that framed a mosaic of the Olympic torch), some bowling trophies. Crunch noticed places where gold and silver paint had been applied to tarnish.

He got up for a moment and read the metal plates on the trophies. They'd been awarded to Meyers himself. Above the trophies were sepia-toned photos of a young Meyers posing with a shiny black bowling ball. Returning to his seat, Crunch noticed the right hand of Ray Meyers, the hand holding the telephone. It only had three fingers on it.

"So where were we?" Meyers said, resting the phone back on its cradle.

"We hadn't really gotten to the point yet."

"Well, all right, let's get to the point. My feeling— and this is a judgment call—is we wait."

"Excuse me?"

"Don't jump at the first offer. I think the potential is huge."

"What are you talking about?"

"I've already had a call from Cronfeld and Fisher; they handle the Rolaids account. They want you...."

"I'm sorry," Crunch said, "but I'm afraid I have got no idea what you're talking about."

"That's why I'm telling you. Since your national debut as a lunatic, you're Madison Avenue's most wanted sports figure in America...."

"Come again?"

"Don't get me wrong. Wheaties ain't breakin' down the door. I mean, you're not exactly the next ambassador of good will. But Miller Light wants you. So does Gillette. Campbell's Soup called about your availability. That's why I'm sayin', wait till the offers *all* roll in, then decide."

"Are you telling me these people want me to do *commercials*?" Crunch was flabbergasted. He'd once done a local spot for Four Corners Lincoln Mercury and had hated it. The makeup felt like wet stucco on his face. The lights made his eyes tear. On the video playback, he had looked mummified.

Mr. Meyers laughed again and ran his hand over his thick, combed back, gray hair. "By the way, have you been fired yet?"

"I don't know. I don't think so. Actually I'm here to try to save my job."

"But you don't know?"

"No, I don't. Has there been anything in the papers?" Crunch asked.

"Just speculation. Some ad agencies feel it would enhance your marketability as the angry college coach if you were fired...."

"Hmm," Crunch mused. "I guess then I wouldn't

need my point guard...."

"If you still have an interest in coaching, the offers will eventually trickle in.... If, on the other hand, you want to do TV color commentary, the offers are gonna start *pouring* in—along with the lecture tours, the six-figure book deals.... Look at John Madden, will ya?"

"So you're saying I should just go ahead and have Four Corners University give me the boot...."

"The million-dollar boot."

"Coaching is my life," Crunch said soberly.

"Do volunteer work with the Boys Clubs of America."

"How much money you figure I can make doing all this?"

Mr. Meyers slipped a gold pen from his breast pocket and wrote on a square-inch of Post-it parchment a number with more zeroes than Crunch cared to count. He stuck the tiny note on Crunch's index finger and said, "Think about it, and get back to me. Soon!"

Crunch stood up; he shook the agent's hand. He felt woozy. He thought about the creature he'd seen an hour ago in the subway station men's room beneath the sink. *Here I am about to be a millionaire for being a lunatic on TV while some other lunatic, for lack of TV coverage, rots with a beehive under his arm.* Crunch walked to the door and grabbed the knob, then turned around. "I've thought about it," he said.

Meyers, who had started to dial a telephone number, dropped his hand from the touch pad and grinned slightly. "You have?"

"And I've decided that what I really want out of

life is not to be an antacid clown or a razor-blade huckster. All I really want right now—the reason I came here in the first place—is for my point guard."

"You came here for a point guard?"

"*My* point guard."

"Mr. Crunch, you realize that all of my clients are professionals."

"All except for one."

Mr. Meyers tensed behind his desk. His face froze, except for his nostrils, which dilated with each breath. "What are you getting at?" he asked grimly.

"I think you know or you wouldn't be so upset right now," Crunch said.

"Upset? I'm upset because I don't like to see a potential client walk away from a small fortune."

"Well, you can't buy me off."

"Nobody's buying you off."

"All right, where's Jerome Straughter?"

"Who?"

"Clauzell Thomas. Where's Clauzell Thomas?"

"Clauzell?" Meyers laughed nervously and shrugged. "He's at camp. He's with the New Jersey Nets."

"No he's not. I saw him two nights ago playing in a church in Brooklyn."

"Why would he be at a church in Brooklyn when I just got him signed with an NBA team?"

"Because it ain't Clauzell Thomas you got signed, that's why…. You're paying Clauzell for the use of his name. Or maybe you didn't even pay him and you just made him some fancy-sounding promise…."

Meyers stood and reached for his intercom. "It's

been nice getting to know you, Mr. Crunch, but I have other business to attend to." Meyers put out his hand for a shake and threw Crunch a look that was supposed to imply: you can leave the easy way or you can leave the hard way.

Crunch showed no fear. "I have a letter of intent from Jerome Straughter," Crunch said. "You have no legal right to sign that boy as a pro."

"That's why I didn't sign him."

"That's why you passed him off as Clauzell Thomas."

Meyers shook his head. "I'm going to have to call building security if you don't leave."

"I can have you arrested for fraud, mister."

"You can't prove anything."

"Oh, yes I can."

"Don't even try it, Crunch. That kid you saw in Brooklyn was an optical illusion. You know what an optical illusion is, Captain Crunch?"

"Yeah, Mr. Meyers. I sure do. It's when one man puffs a lot of smoke in front of the truth to make another man think he's seeing a mirage."

"You aren't going to find Clauzell Thomas playing any more church basketball in Brooklyn. I can guarantee that! Clauzell Thomas is a free agent at the New Jersey Nets training camp. Matter of fact, he's got a good shot at a starting slot. And no one is gonna believe such wild accusations coming from the Buddy Ryan of NCAA basketball!"

Crunch drew in a hard breath. He could still smell the virulent blood of that subway pimp on his blazer. "You pimps are all alike," he said. "I wish to hell I had a hatpin with me." In lieu of that, Crunch reached down and grabbed the edge of Meyers's desk and felt the adrenal strength to hurl it through the window.

Meyers cracked a slow sardonic smile. "I'm a pimp, huh?"

"You'd buy your own mother a new Corvette, then sell her to the Libyans if there was a buck in it for you."

"Well, what do you call someone who would use the God-given talents of a young man to enrich his own won/loss record, use that kid for four years while the kid's weak knees and ankles are deteriorating…?"

Meyers held up his complete left hand along with the three mangled fingers of his right hand. "…so that by the time he gets his chance to make some money, to have a life, he's a cripple?"

"You sonuvabitch!" Crunch lifted the desk. He clean and jerked it up over his head, leaving Mr. Meyers standing in dismay, his head cocked like a puzzled dog. "My players are my family!" Crunch howled. "I only do what's best for them."

Crunch's muscles tensed, ready to spring into action. To hurl that table through the window—and maybe take Mr. Meyers with it. The world would be a better place in which to live. The game of basketball would not miss this parasite.

But then Crunch imagined all the people down on the street, on their way to lunch or whatever. He thought about his former number-four assistant coach, Yule McMahon, and the falling car battery.

Crunch glared at Mr. Meyers's chopped up hand and had a sudden vague recollection of a guy named

Meyers on the pro bowling tour back in the late 1950s who got in trouble with some underworld pin-shading scheme and had his career ended in a suspicious delicatessen accident. Crunch felt a wave of sympathy dilute his rage. "Oh, what's the use!" he sighed and dropped the table behind him—resigned to the mild enjoyment of smashing a lamp and crushing an ashtray.

# 11

## *Hanging onto the Dream*

AS HE SPAT OUT OF the revolving door and into the Avenue of the Americas pedestrian chaos, Captain Crunch was captivated by the sight of a pay telephone shell. He heard the jingle of coins in his pocket and felt for a quarter. He could ask 411 for the number of the local NCAA office, call them, set up a meeting. With any luck their office would be somewhere right up the Avenue of Americas. But when Crunch reached the metallic telephone console, he did not dial 411. He called Four Corners. He called his ex-wife's home and asked to speak to his son, Todd.

"He's not here just now," Margie said, but Crunch could hear the boy's footsteps, in the background, shaking the floors of their jerry-built tract home, crushing his father's spirit.

"Why won't he talk to me?" Crunch asked.

"He thinks you're going to yell at him. He thinks you don't love him. He thinks all you're interested in is prostituting him for the sake of your team."

Crunch sighed. "I kind of wish you wouldn't say that."

"It's the truth, isn't it, Nick?"

"I taught him everything he knows, goddamnit. deserve to have him play for me."

"You see?" Margie said. "That's what I mean."

Crunch pressed his head against the telephone's emergency instructions. "What does Todd want from me?"

"He wants you to take an interest in him as a per son...."

"Christ, Margie, I go to all his games."

"As a father or as a coach?"

"A little of both."

"But you never go to his piano recitals."

"Why should I? He stinks on the piano! He can' even get through one chorus of *Rhapsody In Blu* without hitting a clangor!"

"Exactly." Margie's smug—though all too brief— silence wafted across the wire. "That's the point," sh continued. "If you loved the boy—if you really love the boy you'd savor every last one of those clangors.

"Oh, is that what you and Ed do every night? S around and relish the sound of Todd butchering th *Great American Songbook*?"

Crunch hung up. He didn't slam the phone dow but he did not treat it with much dignity either. H briskly retraced his steps to the subway station and back uptown to Harlem. He felt hollow, bled of his emotions, stung by a residual postpartum depression. He needed very badly to be in the bosom of his family. The best he could do without an airplane ticket (and quite possibly the best he could do *period*) was to enmesh himself within the Straughter family.

As he stood amid the compressed mass within the crosstown IRT shuttle, Crunch anticipated the apartment alive with the vital sounds and sights and smells of children. He'd find a book and read a story or two with a couple of the older tykes, change a diaper or two, and then maybe share a plate of Harlem strawberries with Patricia.

But when he did enter unit 1044 of building number 3 of the Richard M. Nixon Project, Crunch knew immediately that things were not about to go according to plan.

The children—all twelve of them—were miraculously asleep at the same time, strewn out on the furniture and on blankets on the floor. They seemed all to be breathing in unison.

Crunch closed the door quietly behind him and went exploring for a place to sit down. He found Patricia in her tiny bedroom, on the bed, facing the wall and ruminating over a Con-Ed bill. He tiptoed to the bed, snuck up behind her, and puckered up to plant one on her neck—but she turned, suddenly, startling him.

"Mr. Crunch!" she said, gasping. She was back to wearing the scarf and housecoat. With the outfit seemed to go that unassuming air that made Crunch

165

feel like he had just committed a crime.

Was this the same woman he had made love to just yesterday? Considering this, Crunch was overcome with remorse.

"Is something the matter?" Patricia asked, head tilted, eyes peeking up at Crunch, who now stood clumsily against a gold-plated mirror on the wall.

"I'd like to apologize."

"For what?"

"For yesterday."

Patricia looked away. She seemed confused. "Don't worry about a thing. Yesterday's gone."

"Thank you," Crunch said, but he knew that her forgiveness would not amount to any relief inside of him—not until he forgave himself.

"Let me pay that bill for you," Crunch urged.

"After what you're doing for my son Dwayne, I can't accept your money. He's gonna be a doctor, you know."

"Yes, he told me."

"But it's just the fact that you cared. That's what makes me the happiest. That Dwayne's future meant something to you."

Crunch avoided Patricia for the rest of the afternoon—which was not easy within the tiny apartment—and by suppertime his dignity had begun to resurface. Dwayne had come home from work, and Tiffany arrived shortly thereafter. Crunch joined them all around the dinner table, and when Patricia asked Crunch to say grace, his upper spine tingled with emotion.

He didn't know what to say, could remember no

prayers from his childhood—and had said no prayers pertaining to food since becoming an adult. But somehow he muddled through.

Fish sticks, mustard greens, creamed corn, and waffles with gravy were passed around the table. Crunch dug in along with everyone else. He savored each dish, enchanted by the way the different flavors melded together like a well-oiled, high-tempo, halfcourt offense. He particularly got a kick out of the way the greens left a magnetic sensation on his front teeth.

Nobody said very much during the meal. Dwayne did not ask Crunch about the outcome of his meeting with the agent. He seemed a little cheerier than he had that morning, but not by much. That look of resignation—the one Crunch first noticed last night when he met Dwayne at the library—seemed to have begun to settle in around Dwayne's features.

After seconds of everything, Crunch insisted on helping clear the table. In the kitchen, Crunch fed Patricia the dirty dishes as she busted suds at the sink while Dwayne and Tiffany wrapped leftovers.

"Help yourself to some ice cream, Mr. Crunch," she said.

"I'm stuffed. Thanks anyway. Though I wouldn't mind a few of them strawberries from the window."

"Strawberries?" Patricia laughed. "Those aren't for eating. They're just to look at."

"What do you mean?" Crunch asked. "You and me, we had a whole plate of them yesterday…."

This reminder seemed to disturb Patricia, who retreated to the dishwater and her own thoughts. Dwayne tapped Crunch solemnly on the back of the shoulder, and gestured him through the living room and into the bedroom hallway.

"All I did was ask for some strawberries. I'm tellin' you we had a whole plate!"

"They take turns," Dwayne said.

"What are you talkin' about?"

"My mama and Jerome's mama. They take turns."

"Take turns at what?"

"Life...."

"They take turns? You mean I've been living here with two different women?"

Dwayne nodded his head.

"And nobody told me?"

"We try not to make a big deal out of it. It's the way it's always been. They were both married to my father, Jerome's father, only papa didn't know it. They take turns, man. One comes, the other one goes. One grows strawberries on the ledge, the other eats them. Jerome and I, we figured it out, but we never told anybody. Even papa. We were afraid he'd split us up. Man went to his grave believing he was married to one woman."

"One hell of a woman."

"They even changed their names. I checked it out. They used to be named Wanda and Kay. Now, they're both Patricia."

"Isn't that against the law?" Crunch asked. He was less confused now than he had been five minutes ago—but also he was a little outraged. "Where do they go? Where does each of them go when it's not her turn to be here?"

"I don't know," Dwayne said. "It's none of my

business. They were good to me. They were good to Jerome. They never got nasty with us. Whoever was around was around; know what I mean? And papa always said he was a lucky man, although sometimes they drove him crazy."

"No shit," Crunch said. "But I still don't understand. Why don't they just be themselves? Just each be a different person—and grow and eat their own strawberries—and quit confusing everybody?"

The young man shrugged. "Half a life means half the pain."

"It also means half the pleasure."

"Yeah. Maybe it's worth it for some people...."

Crunch pondered this idea as he lay bug-eyed with exhaustion on the sofa late that night. On the one hand, he kind of wished he could take a vacation from his own life—let someone else run the controls for a while. But at the same time he was not at all sure that dodging half the pain was worth losing half the pleasure. For the moment, he felt both acute pleasure and unbearable pain. Every cell of his body felt tranquil and satisfied and yet the sum total of his being still was an intense longing.

Crunch could hear a minor commotion in the kitchen, got up, and found Patricia fighting with the rusted crank of the window. He helped her get it open and then watched as she lifted a plant pot of baby strawberries off the ledge and ran some water over them.

"I didn't mean to be inhospitable, Mr. Crunch. If you really want some, I'll fix you a plate."

"That's all right," Crunch told her. "Sometimes it's

enough just to admire something, to be a spectator. Maybe you appreciate things better when you're in the stands than when you're all freaked out on the sidelines. You know what I mean?"

Patricia—the Patricia he was currently in the company of—tipped the planter from side to side to evenly distribute the water.

"Do you ever want to smell them?" Crunch asked. "Do you ever want to put your nose up to a strawberry and take a whiff?"

"Yeah," she replied, with a bittersweet smile. "Sometimes I do." And she rested the planter back on the ledge.

"Should I close the window?" Crunch asked.

"Halfway, thank you. Close it halfway."

FIRST THING THE NEXT morning, Crunch resumed the controls of his life. He got on the horn and called the New York City office of the NCAA. It answered with a synthesized voice that told the listener to punch the number of the extension he or she wanted—if he or she had a touchtone phone—or else stay on the line and wait for an operator, presumably a live human voice.

When the operator answered, Crunch knew she was live because he couldn't comprehend a word of her greeting.

"Is this the NCAA?" he checked, sitting up straight on the sofa that was his office and his bed.

"Yes, it is…."

"I need to speak with someone about a recruiting violation. It involves an agent."

"I'm sorry, sir, everyone from that department is in Kentucky or Oklahoma or Las Vegas right now. Would you like to leave a message?"

"I need to talk to someone. This is very serious. Is there anyone there with some authority?"

No answer, but then he heard the periodic purr that meant his call was ringing in someone's office.

"Operations, this is Heller."

"Hi, Heller, this is Nick Cruschenctuwitz. Captain Crunch. Head coach at Four Corners...."

"We haven't made a decision yet, Mr. Crunch. Your university will be informed as soon as we do."

"Then you know?"

The voice laughed. "Yes we know."

"And what are you gonna do about it?"

"That's what we're still deciding, sir. This really isn't protocol for you to be contacting us directly over this matter."

"Why the hell not?" Crunch asked. "I mean what the hell are you people there for?"

"Mr. Crunch, I wouldn't get testy if I were you— at least not until after we've announced your penalty."

"*My* penalty."

"For attacking Hal Beckett."

"Oh, *that* penalty," Crunch said, laughing uneasily. "Look, tell everyone I'll donate some time to the war on drugs.... I'll do a speaking tour. I'll make some videos about how to get high on life. I'll even go to Miami and sniff luggage on behalf of collegiate athletics. But that's not what I've called about, Mr. Heller. I want to report a recruiting violation."

"I'm afraid that department…."

"I know they're all tied up playing golf with Eddie Sutton and tennis with Billy Tubbs, but I've gotta talk to them."

"What are the nature of your allegations?"

Crunch conveyed the nature of his allegations to Mr. Heller, who whistled in awe.

"I need immediate action," Crunch said.

"I understand," Heller said. "Of course, we'll have to see some kind of proof."

"Proof of what?"

"That the player in question—the one who signed with the Nets—really is the one who signed your letter of intent."

"I know it is. I'm telling you, I found the real Clauzell Thomas at a church in Brooklyn."

"Can you bring him to my office? I have an opening tomorrow at three-thirty, or else the middle of next week…."

"Now I gotta go looking for Clauzell Thomas all over New York?"

"We need some kind of proof to back up your allegations against Mr. Meyers. We've never found any improprieties with regard to Mr. Meyers before…."

"You've got my word. I'll sign a sworn statement as to his unscrupulous activities. Doesn't that mean anything?"

"At the moment?"

"I guess not," Crunch said. "I guess when a coach loses his cool like any normal human being and expresses his disapproval for lousy officiating, I guess he just isn't worthy of anybody's trust. I guess he

172

might as well go coach girls' volleyball."

"Mr. Cruschenctuwitz, the NCAA doesn't have the resources to investigate every allegation of recruiting violations."

"Yeah, yeah," Crunch said, irritated—though it did occur to him that, yes, if the NCAA did have the resources to investigate every allegation of recruiting violations that he'd probably have been banned from coaching fifteen years ago, along with many of his esteemed colleagues. "But can't you just come with me to the New Jersey Nets's training camp?"

"Not without some kind of evidence."

"Evidence.... You want some goddamned evidence?"


"PACK YOUR BAGS," Crunch commanded moments later, bursting into Dwayne's room and flipping on the lights. "We're going to New Jersey."

"What for?" Dwayne asked groggily.

"What do you think? To find Jerome."

Crunch stood still in the doorway for several dead minutes. His eyes tracked the four walls. Each wore fresh white paint, but they still seemed to be closing in on one another. The only furniture was an elevated bed with a built-in desk and shelves beneath it— the whole thing made of painted scrap lumber. Dwayne did not move from the bed.

Captain Crunch, not wanting to be intrusive, remained in the doorway and addressed the soles of Dwayne's shoes. "I'm hoping we can talk some sense into your cousin once we get there," Crunch said. "But it would help if we had some kind of physical evidence."

Dwayne said nothing; his foot twitched against the wall.

"Tell me, was Jerome ever fingerprinted?"

"No."

"I didn't mean anything by that. I'm not saying your cousin was ever in trouble with the law or anything like that. Sometimes they just fingerprint kids for the hell of it."

Dwayne's foot flexed, the knuckles crackling.

"No fingerprints, huh?"

"Uh-uh."

"Any birthmarks or other distinguishing marks on his body that you know of?"

"Why don't you ask his mother?"

"I already did; I mean, I asked one of your mothers. I don't remember which one I asked. Let's just say I asked a woman named Patricia."

"Then I guess you'd know if Jerome had any distinguishing birthmarks."

"As a matter of fact I don't know shit. Are there any dental records of Jerome?"

"I don't know."

"Who's his dentist?"

"I don't now."

"Who's *your* dentist?"

"I don't have one."

"You've never been to the dentist?"

"I don't remember."

"I think you do," Crunch said, stepping into the room and finding Dwayne's eyes just above the ridge of his mattress. "And I think you know who your cousin's dentist is."

"Leave me alone."

"Would you like me to come back in an hour?"

"No, I wouldn't."

Crunch backed up an inch or two and felt the wall behind him. "Dwayne? Are you trying to tell me the deal is off?"

"Is that all you care about?" Dwayne asked.

"No, it's not. But I need to know."

"Well, why don't *you* tell *me* if the deal's off," Dwayne said.

"Are you gonna help me find your cousin?"

Dwayne rolled over and faced the wall, leaving Crunch with his back and his shadow. "No, I'm not going to help you."

"Why not?"

"I've been thinking about it, and...I've already betrayed him, trying to get over. I can't betray my brother any more."

"He's not your brother," Crunch said, at a loss. "He's your cousin.... I mean, he's your *half*-brother...."

"He's family."

That stung. It was a lousy deal, Crunch thought, to have to make your own family a patchwork of friendly strangers and have to find out the feeling isn't mutual. He wished he could, just for the moment, think fondly about his own son without at the same time getting so pissed at Todd's mother and at Todd himself and at Dean Smith.

"You haven't betrayed Jerome," Crunch offered to Dwayne numbly. "You did what you felt was best for

175

him at the time."

"Wrong. I was thinkin' 'bout myself."

"It doesn't matter what you were thinkin' about, son. You still did the right thing. Hell, sometimes scientists set out to cure one disease and wind up with a cure for another. What we're doin' for Jerome is for his own good. We've got to save Jerome from the clutches of that Madison Avenue pimp."

"It's not *we* anymore, coach."

Crunch heard the front door open, heard Tiffany's voice in the front room, chattering with Patricia— happy sounds, sounds of exasperation and exhaustion, but happy exhaustion along with the lovely smell of donuts and coffee and fresh styrofoam. He wanted more than anything to be a part of it. "I wish you'd think it over, son."

"I'm not your son."

"I know.... I'm sorry. I meant it in a nice way."

"I believe you did. I really do. It's been nice knowing you, coach."

Crunch supposed he should leave now. He started through the doorway.

"No hard feelings," Dwayne said. "I know you're just doing your job, Captain Crunch. I understand that."

"Bullshit!" Crunch exploded, bracing himself against the doorway molding. "If you think all I'm here for is to do a job, then you do *not* understand." On the word "not" he punched one of the four-by-fours supporting the bed.

"I'm sorry I got myself involved, Captain Crunch. I made a mistake. Please leave me alone."

"No, I won't just leave you alone. I can't do that."

"It'll be easier than you think."

"I care about you."

"What for?" Dwayne asked. "I don't play ball."

"You're young, you're talented—at whatever it is you do—and you've got a dream."

"Not anymore."

Crunch shook the bed. "Don't say that. You know goddamn well you've got a dream. Hold on to that fuckin' dream. And go after it!"

"I can't. Not if the dream is going to make me a back-stabber."

"Ah, shit, man, don't talk that way. Wake up, Dwayne. This is the real world. You can't tiptoe out of the gutter."

"That's right."

"Well then make some noise! Quit minding your own business! Don't you give up, Dwayne Straughter. You can get to college."

"I'm not gonna help you, Captain Crunch. No matter what you say or how you say it, I'm not your ace anymore."

Crunch, his hand leaning on a piece of the bed, felt it tremble. He saw Dwayne's body wriggle slightly. He thought the kid was laughing. "It's not funny," he said and then realized the kid was crying.

"I guess I've overstayed my welcome," Crunch said and walked out.

Passing the two ladies and their donuts and coffee, he winked casually, as if stepping out for some air. He wanted to make a stab at goodbye—*"Say hello to your other half for me"*—but feared he'd end up making a fool of himself.

Out on the street, it took a while to find an operable pay phone. When he did, Crunch, armed with his AT&T calling card, phoned Kurt Crane at Mid-Atlantic Reliable Health Insurance Underwriters. He was amazed that the COO and Posse alumnus was still accessible for the needs of the now infamous Captain Crunch.

"I need some information."

"Information?"

"If it isn't too much trouble," Crunch intoned. "I need to know who Jerome Straughter's dentist is."

"Why? You wanna make sure your point guard has a good bite?"

Crunch didn't think that was funny, but he figured he'd better stay on Kurt's good side with an enthusiastic laugh; he ended up laughing too hard and sounding phony and tried to cough his way out of it. This attracted the attention of some Puerto Rican teenagers on a nearby stoop who made fun of him in two different languages. Seeing this, Crunch deemed it was time to shut up and stand still.

"Are you serious?" Crane asked. "You need dental X-rays?"

"If there's any way you can find them, I'd be very appreciative."

"Where can I reach you?" Kurt asked.

"I'm going to New Jersey. Princeton, New Jersey. I'll call and give you the motel number when I get there."

"Super," Kurt said, but Crunch was not optimistic. He kept putting himself on Kurt's end of the conversation and figured he'd better explain: "I think I've found Jerome Straughter, but I've got to prove it's him. He's never been fingerprinted and no one will tell me if he has any birthmarks."

"Sure," Kurt said.

"Really. I swear it's the truth."

"I know you do."

"I'm not crazy."

"Of course not."

Just then, Crunch felt a sharp jab at the base of his back. He heard a thick mumble: "Up d'cash, muh-fa. This a strap. I ain't 'fraid to smoke yo ass."

Crunch reached into his front pocket for his wallet. He reached slowly, ambivalently. Without his cash and credit cards—and now that he had all but demolished his reputation and lost most of his connections— Crunch feared what would become of him. He might wind up under a sink with a beehive growing from his arm.

He could hear the mugger sniffling powerfully behind his head, could hear the Puerto Rican teenagers gassing on his dilemma:

"*Que vas hacer, viejo?*"

"Don't be a *maricon*…. Fight!"

He recalled a conversation between two Posse forwards during a bus ride to Brigham Young. One player, Griffith Charles, who hailed from northeast Washington, D.C., was explaining to Brian Moret, a white boy from rural Nebraska, the best way to avoid bodily harm when confronted with a weapon in the inner city.

"Get crazy," Griffith Charles had said. "Nobody

179

wants to deal wit' no nut. Get that psycho gleam in yo eye, start droolin' or some shit. Have epilepsy if you have to."

With that in mind, Crunch turned his head, psyched himself up for a tongue swallowing seizure—but that wasn't necessary. Crunch already had that psycho gleam in his eye—he'd had it, off and on, for the past three weeks—and as soon as the mugger saw the harried face of Captain Crunch, he backed up, pivoted forty-five degrees, and then bolted across the street.

"Hey, wait," Crunch hollered. "Can you tell me where a man can get a crowbar around here?"

"Yeah, old man," said one of the Puerto Ricans on the stoop—a girl in a halter top that was a modified pair of men's jockey shorts and some baggy fatigue pants, from which she somehow produced a large black crowbar. "*Pesa de mucho para usar como una caña*! Wha-you gonna do wid it, grampa?"

Crunch noticed an immense disparity between how he would like to have responded to that question and the manner which he deemed safe. "I'll give you ten bucks for it," he said.

"Fifteen," the girl said.

"Make it twenty."

STILL EARLY IN THE MORNING, the Adam Clayton Powell Memorial Yard was quiet, except for the light hum of cars passing in waves on either side. Holding the crowbar low to the ground, like it might be the fortified leash of an invisible dog, Crunch scouted the turf. He was completely alone. A strange feeling, having had no solitude since arriving in New

York—except for those hours in the elephant shit room at Madison Square Garden. Flocks of pigeons swooped down occasionally to sift through the debris of food wrappers, beer cans, whiskey bottles, discarded narcotics paraphernalia, mangled flashlight batteries, solidified vomit, and a twin-sized mattress that seemed to have been cut in half with a chain saw.

Captain Crunch walked to the center of the basketball court. The footprints and handprints were still there, along with Jerome Straughter's signature. With his eyes and his own size ten-and-a-half Hush Puppies, Crunch measured a six-inch radius from the goods and drew an ellipse in his mind, then pounded out the edges with the crowbar's claw until the asphalt crumbled in a shape that was not quite the ellipse he'd set out to carve out—it looked more like an enlarged ink dot.

Crunch turned the crowbar so that its flat end was down. He plunged the hard flat metal into the cracked asphalt, then tilted the neck of the crowbar down and stood up on it until Jerome Straughter's signature and prints rose up out of the ground like a hot muffin on a spatula.

Captain Crunch looked around to see if anyone was watching. The only human eyes he could make out were those inside the cars on the Harlem River Drive—and they were intent on the road with seemingly no peripheral interest.

# 12

## *Every Team Needs a Role Player*

FROM HIS WINDOW SEAT inside the Jersey bound Greyhound, Crunch's last impressions of New York City were sad. Narrow crowded streets, standing still. Dented cars and people with sagging heads, their eyes sluggishly following the moving bus. The smell of a lone Italian sausage sizzling on an old man's lunch cart. The final curtain of Crunch's adventures in the Big Apple was the piss-colored tile on the walls inside the Holland Tunnel.

"Are you a sculptor?" asked a young white girl sitting next to him.

"Huh?" Crunch shifted his eyes without moving his head.

"I'm an art major at Princeton," she said. "I thought

you might be a sculptor." Her eyes aimed at the large slab of cement beneath the seat in front of Captain Crunch—his carry-on luggage.

Unable to conceive of another explanation—and not in the mood to emit enough hostility to get the girl to leave him alone—Crunch said, "Yeah, I'm a sculptor."

"Can I see your work?"

"You want to *see* it?"

"Yeah. I've worked with marble and clay but never cement. Is that what that is?"

"Yeah, that's what it is."

"Can I see?"

Lacking the strength to mount a defense, Crunch reached down for the slab. It seemed heavier now than when he'd excavated it from the Adam Clayton Powell Yard. He couldn't imagine how he'd lugged it all the way to the subway, then downtown to Port Authority.

The girl admired the jagged edges, as if they'd been carefully carved. "What tool did you use to get this effect?" she asked.

"A crowbar," Crunch said.

"Wow!"

She looked at the top surface, at the footprints and handprints and the crude signature of Jerome Straughter. "What's it called?" she asked.

"What do you mean?"

"This piece. Does it have a name?"

"A Mind is a Terrible Thing to Waste," Crunch said.

"Interesting. I like that."

Crunch enjoyed this charade. Yes, he was a sculptor, on his way to lecture at Princeton on the merits of vandalizing city property for the sake of art.

He looked around him at the other passengers. Mostly students. Soft faces—except for a few boys whose faces were ravaged with acne—all of them at ease with their textbooks and their newspapers and their bright-eyed conversations and their unburdened laughter. It would have cheered him up; it would have made him feel right about himself and the world for a minute or two, except that he kept thinking about Dwayne Straughter, hiding up on his suspended scrap wood bed, crying into the blank white wall of his room.

Hoping to escape those nagging memories, Crunch asked his neighbor if he could borrow the sports section of her *USA Today*. He found the pre-conference college hoop box scores. The Posse had lost again, this time to Moab City College. *USA Today*'s Division-One rankings had now dropped Four Corners from number 18 to number 31 to number 97—the lowest the Posse had sunk since Crunch had become their coach more than twenty years ago. Crunch tried to detach himself.

It's just a game, he thought. It's about ticket sales and TV rights and concessions. It's about how many Four Corners Posse players make a future impact in the NBA so we can sell "Lynch Mob" sweatshirts at our campus bookstore, at the Four Corners Stuckey's, at O'Hare Airport, Fisherman's Wharf, Miami Beach, and your neighborhood K-Mart store.

Crunch slid Jerome Straughter's fifty-pound ID

back under the seat in front of him. He studied the box score and mused.

"Moab City College...."

He had to laugh. Even with Jerome Straughter in the backcourt, Crunch was no longer so sure the Posse would win their conference, much less do any serious damage in the March field of sixty-four.

THEN, A FEW HOURS later, he saw Jerome play.

It was about twenty minutes into the evening practice of the New Jersey Nets. Crunch had already checked into the Garden State Motel, cleaned up, rented a subcompact car, and driven to the Princeton campus. He'd left Jerome Straughter's foot and hand prints in the car's trunk.

Security was tight at the Nets training facility, but fortunately one of the free agents trying to make their squad was Milt Powdell, once a power forward with the Posse, and Milt sneaked the coach in, no questions asked. The old Jadwin Gym was virtually empty. Mostly players, coaches, trainers. The only spectators other than Crunch were a pair of kids sitting a few feet away. The boy and girl both had springy hair, skin the color of lightly varnished furniture, and freckled faces. They smelled intensely of bubble gum.

Tony Kitchen, the massive coach of the Nets, stood before his players with his clipboard and his assistants. Immediately, Crunch could tell which players enjoyed guaranteed contracts (the guys yawning and clowning) and which players were scrapping to make the team (the guys standing at the front, drinking up Kitchen's every word). Crunch was again flushed with cynicism about organized basketball—the NBA in particular, which had a dubious place in Crunch's heart:

Here are these guys, supposed to be formed into a team, and yet half of them hate the other half for trying to take away their jobs. The pros with guaranteed money—the stars and the solid contributors and the defensive specialists—they aren't wearing this uniform because they got some affinity for the state of New Jersey or for Tony Kitchen or for each other. They may stand up and tell the scribes how it's a team effort and they'll do whatever has to be done for the good of the team, but they're only with this team because this team is willing to pay them more money than the other teams. And when their current contract expires, if someone *does* offer a sweeter deal, they'll do the bird—they'll put on another uniform and sing platitudes about doing what's best for the team, the new team, as long as that team is spitting out the paychecks.

So where is the real game of NBA basketball played?

Is winning really decided on the ninety-four-foot hunk of wood? Or at the negotiating table of the Avenue of the American Pimps?

Crunch continued to tell himself that he did not care—that it was all a farce—as the anticipation of the scrimmage mounted within him. He didn't even notice Jerome Straughter, whose face was obscured by a scraggly mustache and beard and blended into the assemblage of sweating bodies near the midcourt stripe.

Then the first dribble echoed through the rafters of the hallowed gymnasium—and Jerome emerged instantly.

He was even better than the crude videotapes Crunch had scouted. He was better than Crunch had ever imagined in his most vivid and outrageous fantasies.

Jerome Straughter moved up and down the court like some exotic feline. He dribbled with the control of a kid spinning a yo-yo and moved laterally as if on ice skates. His first trip down the floor on offense, Jerome spun two defenders around with one stutter step and a brutal headfake, then sliced into the lane. Two big men converged on him—and he flipped the ball to an open teammate for an easy deuce.

His impact on the scrimmage was immediate and it was profound. From that first play on, when the ball was in his hands, the other nine guys spun around him like electron clouds around an atomic nucleus; even when he made a pass he remained a magnetic charge, the eye of the whirlpool. The other players, as they set screens, muscled low, and made cuts, their eyes were glued—at least peripherally—to Jerome. They knew he would reward them, feed them the ball in the right spot the instant they got some daylight. And he did.

Jerome made his teammates play over their heads. He made them do things Crunch had never seen them do before in any of the Nets games he'd seen on Superstation TNT: hit shots they didn't usually hit, fill the wings on the fast break; he even got them in a rhythm that had them in good position to clear the

188

offensive boards. In short, Jerome Straughter made this bunch of overpaid, oversexed, complacent ego-maniacs into a fluid, honed machine, a spirited team with a survivalist attitude.

As cool as Jerome Straughter ran his offense, he was that frenzied on defense (a pleasant surprise considering his "offense only" scouting rep). He was a helter-skelter kamikaze and had his teammates playing the same way: hands up, arms flailing, eyes gyrating, toes planted—anticipating—hips jerking sporadically, unnerving the man with the ball.

Jerome just plain *owned* the tempo on the court. When he slowed, the game slowed. When he put it in high gear, pushing the ball up court, the kinetic energy on the floor increased with him. He made steals, he made no-look passes in midair. He had eyes in the back of his head, in the side of his head, on top of his head. When the defense sagged off, he nailed the J; when they pressured him, he penetrated; when they double-teamed, he dished.

Captain Crunch began to drool. His eyes teared up from staring hypnotically at Jerome, and from a twitch of awe.

It doesn't get any better than this, Crunch thought. He seemed to be floating above the aluminum bleachers. He felt intoxicated and he felt queasy. He was in love. The man was in love!

Tony Kitchen's whistle shrilled; Crunch jumped. He swung his head around, thinking someone had blown it right in his ear. Man, did he ever hate that sound. Even when it was Crunch himself blowing the tiny silver instrument at the Posse, it made him cringe;

189

it made him think about the dreaded referees. Kitchen made substitutions. Jowls radiating, he yanked Jerome from the game and patted him on the rump. Tony Kitchen didn't need to see any more. He too was in love.

Crunch, despite his utmost respect for Tony Kitchen—as a retired player and as a brave coach—felt the sudden urge to run out on the court and slug him and say, "Leave my point guard alone. He's mine." But he suppressed his jealousy, even as Jerome slung his arm up and around Kitchen's shoulder and tilted his ear upward for a compliment.

Beside Crunch, the freckle-faced boy and girl broke into spontaneous cheers. They stomped their feet, rattling the bleachers and Crunch's nerves. Crunch turned, annoyed—but seeing the iridescent boy and girl screaming, "Go, Dad; go, Dad!" he lost his venom. He smiled at the kids, who couldn't have been more than ten years old. They smiled back.

"Which one's your dad?" he asked, then looked back down at the court and realized the question was a stupid one. There were ten guys on the floor. Eight of them were under twenty-five. One was about twenty-eight. The other guy had a receding afro that had a coarse, dyed look to it. Crunch couldn't figure out who this six-foot-ten over-the-hill stiff was. He was too old to be a rookie or a borderline free agent—by the time a guy is that age he's either made it or he hasn't! Maybe the guy was an assistant coach trying to stay in shape. He waved to the boy and girl, then returned his attention to the impending scrimmage.

"That's our dad," the girl said, her mouth puffy, her

teeth wrapped in braces.

"What's his name?" Crunch asked.

"Gus," the boy beamed. "Gus Anderson Jo."

"Gus Anderson Jo?" Crunch mused. *Didn't Gus Anderson Jo retire eight years ago after a lackluster stint in the NBA?* "I remember your father when he was a center for Al McGuire at Marquette."

The boy adjusted his New York Mets baseball cap and shrugged. His sister nodded. "Dad has a trophy and everything. He graduated from there but he says it's just not enough to have a regular college degree. You still can't make any money except basketball."

Crunch tried to remember Gus. The Posse had played Marquette once during Gus's tenure. But Crunch's memory could not distinguish between Gus and two other big guys on McGuire's team. Even in college Gus was a journeyman. A big body. Five fouls to give. Now, in the NBA, he was six fouls to give. Crunch could not believe this guy was still in the league—and yet, he kept thinking he'd heard some recent news about Gus, something of significance.

"Your father wasn't with the Nets last year was he?" Crunch asked.

Both kids shook their heads. "He was playing for a team in Italy," the girl said. "In a place called Milan."

"We never got to see him," the boy reported. He took out a roll of cherry Life Savers and flicked one in his mouth. "Mom says it's too far for a visit. At least when Dad played in the Continental Basketball Association for Wyoming we got to see him once in a while…."

191

The girl rolled her eyes. "Nobody's interested, Scott," she said, punching the boy.

"That's not true," Crunch said, emphatically. "Your dad's a fine player. He gives his all—and everybody cares about a guy who gives his two hundred percent. That's what a coach looks for."

"Yeah," the boy said and stuck his tongue out at his sister, who jabbed him in the ribs.

"You're nice kids," Crunch said. "You must really love your father."

The girl smiled. The boy blushed a deep purple hue.

Crunch blushed right back, astonished, embarrassed. He couldn't help but remember vaguely what it felt like to be loved this devotedly by Todd. It was a wonderful and scary sensation, as he recalled. One particular moment became vivid in his memory—a strange choice, he thought at first. It was a Sunday morning in the parking lot of a motel near the Grand Canyon. Crunch was loading the suitcases and other trappings of their vacation into the trunk of his Pontiac. It took nearly an hour to fit everything in. Todd watched in awe. Crunch could have spent the rest of his life loading up that car and would have been happy.

Little things, Crunch realized, were the glue of a father and his son. Whereas, the glue that bonded a coach and his players was, sadly, something that had to be earned and was sometimes hard to come by— like winning games, taking conference titles, going all the way….

Coach Kitchen blew the whistle again and the scrimmage resumed. Without Jerome on the floor, the play was inconsistent, sloppy, and, worst of all, dull. Crunch tried to modify the tedium by following the moves of Gus Anderson Jo, cheering and groaning along with the kids as their father lumbered up and down the hardwood, clawing for a job. The man dove for loose balls, sacrificed his equilibrium to draw the charging foul, and made an occasional awkward shot from short range—trying to be the crafty veteran and not be a step behind—trying, it seemed apparent, to sell himself to the coaching staff as a role player, a stable influence for the more talented youngsters.

"You don't think he's playing *too* good do you?" the boy asked.

Crunch laughed.

The boy did not. "If he plays too good some other team might want to make a trade for him...."

"How 'bout if he was traded to the Lakers? Wouldn't you like to live in California?" Crunch asked, winking.

"We wouldn't live in California. We would still be living here in New Jersey with our mother," the boy bemoaned.

"Oh...." Crunch patted the boy on his back. "Well, I wouldn't worry. I think the Lakers have enough big men right now."

Coach Kitchen blew a time-out, and the boy and girl hopped down the bleachers until they reached the court and hugged their dad while he caught his breath and squirted his tongue with Gatorade.

Crunch glanced over at the object of his own affection: Jerome was leaning over a water fountain, splashing his face and wringing out his beard. Jerome jogged, kicking high, around the gym. He passed Gus and the two kids—and then seeing them all at the same time, it hit Crunch: the trade! The massive and complex trade that had brought Clauzell Thomas (the real Jerome Straughter) to the New Jersey Nets had also—for whatever bizarre reason—brought them Gus Anderson Jo.

CRUNCH LEFT THE PRACTICE early, hoping to make a quiet departure. Outside, the chirping night birds, for a split second, made Crunch think he was surrounded by cheap telephones. He found the locker room exit and reparked his car within its view. He had been having a hell of a time getting the key out of the ignition and did not, at that moment, feel like enduring the ordeal of contorting his body beneath the steering column in order to press a certain button while twisting the key toward the dashboard and then pulling it out without letting go of the button. Instead he turned on the radio and found an all-night sports show broadcast, with a high-C background hum, out of New York City.

He had to move his car twice—he was blocking a truck delivering textbooks to the nearby campus bookstore; then he was in the way of a van picking up dirty uniforms from the Princeton rugby team.

Finally, at 11:00 P.M., the locker room exit swung open and the Nets began to trickle out. The first to emerge was Gus Anderson Jo. He wore a black satin Cinzano jacket. His two children, along with a stunning olive-skinned lady, ran to his arms. Then, two and three at a time, came the younger players, some clad in jogging suits, others in torn dungarees and polo shirts. From inside his rented auto, Crunch could not distinguish the black faces and had to shine his low beams to see that Jerome was not among them.

Jerome was the last player out. He was decked out in some white slacks and a green fishnet shirt Crunch remembered from the racks of Kim's Fashions. To Crunch's dismay, Jerome was accompanied by coach Tony Kitchen. Crunch watched them stride to a large Oldsmobile. Kitchen opened the passenger door. He appeared to offer Jerome a ride. Jerome appeared to gracefully decline.

Crunch sighed with relief. He watched Jerome highstep past him, then started the engine and followed the young man. Crunch kept the headlights off so as not to alarm Jerome, but the sound of the engine seemed to make Jerome glance repeatedly over his shoulder and put his strut into high gear.

Crunch stopped the car and slid out of the driver's seat. He tried to quickly disengage the ignition key and wound up twisting his wrist. He tried again and, in his haste, almost pitched his head into the windshield. Seeing Jerome disappear into the darkness of the campus, Crunch abandoned the car and its key and ran. "Jerome," he screamed, and the young man turned around.

"It's me. It's Captain Crunch."

The young man's face tightened. The ends of his beard sharpened. He twirled himself around and kept walking. Crunch went after him.

"Let's talk. Jerome, let's talk."

"Who you talkin' to?"

"You, Jerome Straughter."

Still walking: "That ain't my name. I don't know who you talkin' to."

"Come on, man. You gotta remember me. I'm Captain Crunch. Four Corners University. I know we've never met, but we've spoken on the telephone, and I know you've received my letters and the *Posse Cage Newsletter*. You're a member of the Four Corners Posse, young man...." Crunch offered the young man a handshake.

Jerome left Crunch hanging. He looked at him warily and said, "You the dude that stuffed a whistle down the ref's throat an' put him in a coma. That's all I know about you. From TV. Me, I'm Clauzell Thomas. Ain't got nothin' to say to you."

Still moving, huffing the words out, Crunch said: "I still have your letter of intent, Jerome. I can get you suspended from the NBA."

Jerome stopped walking and turned around. His mouth was cocked with hostility; his eyes glistened with fear.

"Face it, son. You belong to me.... I mean...." Crunch didn't like the sound of that but he didn't know how to revise it and still make his point.

"I didn't sign nothin'," Jerome said.

"There were witnesses, Jerome. You signed it. Your mother signed it—one of them, at any rate. I know what happened to you. An agent named Ray Meyer tracked you down. He said you could make two hundred thousand dollars right now—or was it three hundred thou?"

"I ain't know what you talkin' 'bout."

"Mr. Meyers told you that you were good enough for the pros," Crunch supposed. "And maybe he was right—but that ain't that point. That agent is trying to prostitute you. I'm here to set you free...."

The young man stopped walking. His lower lip curled as if he was about to cry. Then his face hardened. "My name ain't Jerome. My name is Clauzell Thomas. If you got a letter from Jerome somebody or other it don't mean shit t'me. I'm Clauzell, you understand?"

"Why'd you answer when I said Jerome?"

"What it mean?"

"It means you're Jerome."

"Don't mean shit. I'm Clauzell."

Crunch cracked his knuckles. He needed to get the juices flowing in his bones and in his brains. He was beginning to lose heart against this kid's persistent rejection. "You're being sold out, kid. That agent is robbing you the opportunity of an education."

"I'm Clauzell Thomas. I been to college. Georgetown Hoyas. John Thompson a genius."

"You've done your homework," Crunch said. "You're doing a good job, Jerome. You really are. It isn't that you botched this charade either. It's that I never gave up. You're my point guard from heaven, Jerome. I risked my life—I even put my *career* on the line—to have you, Jerome. And I have proof that you are Jerome."

"My name is Clauzell!"

"I've got a piece of cement that says you're not, Jerome. From the Adam Clayton Powell Yard with your footprints and your handprints. Tomorrow morning, I walk into the Princeton athletic department and find Sam Koner, the president. He's inner-circle with the NCAA. He'll be very interested in my matching your limbs with those prints. So why don't you come with me now and save us all a lot of headaches and save yourself some embarrassment and a whole lot of legal trouble?"

"My name is Clauzell," Jerome offered sadly, limply. "Where you got this piece of cement?"

"In my car," Crunch said, "wanna see it?"

"Where's your car?"

Crunch pointed.

"I don't see no car."

Neither did Crunch, not until the inside of the car lit up. The car door was open and someone was in the passenger seat, leaning into the backseat, seemingly searching for something.

"Hey!" Crunch hollered. "Hey, it's a rented car, you asshole. There's nothing in there!"

The engine started.

"Hey! No!"

The white reverse lights glared; the car moved backwards. Crunch dove into a running stride but before he'd accomplished two steps, the subcompact slammed, trunk first, into a delivery truck. A hollow bending sound gave way to a low boom, then a mammoth inanimate cough. The car screeched forward about ten feet, then slammed back into the truck. The car's trunk was now a retracted accordion. Its lid cracked open and asphalt dust rose into the night air.

Crunch's eyes slammed shut. The air around him seemed to tremble.

Jerome was holding back laughter, Crunch was sure. *Go ahead!* Crunch thought. *Laugh at Captain Crunch. I'm an asshole. I deserve this. Have your laugh. You won.*

But the kid didn't laugh. He put his arm around Crunch's shoulder. It was not a gleeful arm, not a mocking arm. It was a warm arm, a caring arm. It patted Crunch with consolation. "Hey, don't take it so hard, coach. I'm sorry it ain't worked out for you. I really am. You gonna be all right, man. You gonna land on your toes. Just got t'roll with the punches."

"Thanks, kid," Crunch said, thinking, not only is he a floor general, he's also a role player with leadership qualities.

Crunch reached out to give the young man's shoulder an affectionate squeeze, to touch him in some way—but Jerome had slipped away. Crunch could hear the fading rubber klop of his footsteps.

# 13

## *Loyalty*

"YOU SONUVABITCH!" Crunch screamed, running toward the mangled rent-a-car, seeing that the thief and vandal was stuck, unable to disengage his seat-belt.

What kind of criminal buckles up? Crunch wondered.

"Dwayne!"

"Yeah, that's right," said Jerome's half-brother, still jerking on the buckle of the unsafe safety belt.

Crunch was stymied. A visceral need to commit homicide sent him lurching, headfirst, into the car and choking Dwayne. "What the fuck are doin' here?"

"What do you think?" Dwayne gagged, his long sharp fingers poking Crunch's eyes.

"What did I ever do to you?" Crunch asked, squeezing harder at the young man's throat.

Dwayne's words were barely audible. "Nothing personal, Captain Crunch," he said, his palm now crushing Crunch's nose and pushing Crunch's head into the rearview mirror. "This was just something I had to do."

Dwayne's face was now a shade of burgundy. The veins in his eyes seemed to be moving like bands of electricity. He jumped up in his seat and, somehow, drove Crunch's head into the glove compartment and then slid out of the choke-hold.

"Something you had to do?" Crunch raged breathlessly, grabbing Dwayne by the hair.

"I heard what you did," Dwayne gasped. "Cat said somebody tore up the Powell Yard…, the full court…. Jerome's signification. I knew it was you!"

Crunch, now entangled in the broken seatbelt, lost much of his homicidal drive—and his energy. Dwayne was a lot tougher than Crunch would have expected.

"I did what I had to do," Crunch said.

"You think the mayor is going to send somebody up to repair the court?"

"Shut up…."

"I thought you loved sandlot basketball—you said that was the way the game was meant to be played. You called it poetry in motion, and then you tore up the fuckin' court so nobody can play—or so some fool will bust up his knee."

"I said shut up!" Crunch tried to grab Dwayne's mouth and hold it shut, but there was too much perspiration—on his hands and on the young man's

202

chin—to get any kind of grip.

"I will not shut up, Captain Crunch."

"Well, then just leave me alone," Crunch said.

"As soon as you help me out of this straitjacket."

Crunch tumbled out of the car and onto the cold pavement. He glanced up at the crushed automobile; it looked like a gigantic piece of shrapnel. "I oughtta leave you in here to rot," Crunch said, leaning over and fiddling with the belt lock. He allowed all of his present frustrations to zero in on this stubborn seat-belt. He stood up and sank his teeth into the shoulder strap and chewed like a beaver until he'd severed it completely. Dwayne slipped up out of the lap belt and hopped out of the car.

"Well, it was nice seein' you," Crunch said with a sickened smile. "Next time we'll have to have lunch...."

"You shouldn't have gotten me involved," Dwayne said. "You should never have made me betray my brother."

"You got bus fare back to New York?"

"I got a return ticket."

"Well, here...." Crunch opened his wallet and peeled out two fifties. "Hire someone to fix the yard." Crunch nodded toward the trunk in which lay the asphalt crumbs and dust that were once Jerome's positive identification. "I'll put that in a sack for you if you want to use it—though I can tell you it's a hell of a load to carry."

"Keep your money," Dwayne said, showing Crunch his back and walking away.

"Wait...." Crunch ran after him. "You done right.

I gotta admit it, and I just want you to know. I still wish you hadn't done what you done, but it was right. Now, for chrissakes, tell Jerome. Tell him how it was you that helped him out. He owes you, Dwayne. Make him pay your college tuition with some of those NBA bucks he's gonna have rolling in."

"He doesn't owe me anything."

"Fine, but make him do it anyway."

"Leave me alone!" And Dwayne ran away.

"No, Dwayne," Crunch hollered. "You deserve to have a life. Not this *half* shit like your mothers. You deserve a *whole* life—all to yourself."

CRUNCH DIDN'T WANT to test the loyalty of anyone at Divine Airlines (and he remained concerned about the possibility of a pilots' strike and some hypertensive Divine executive flying the aircraft), so when he arrived back at his motel room he phoned a business called "We're Your Ticket-24 Hour Travel." When Sally, his eager "travel consultant" asked, "How many will be traveling?" Crunch replied, with the stiff pride of a jilted lover, "One. Just me."

All flights to Arizona, New Mexico, Colorado, and Utah were booked solid for the next few days. He would have to wait for a cancellation. In the meantime, he reported the car accident to Discount Auto Rentals and thought about calling Four Corners. He was anxious to get back to his team—if they still were his team. But he thought he'd better just show up and throw his pitiful self at the mercy of his longtime friend, Dean Kimble.

He collapsed on the bed and closed his eyes. He

figured he'd need about forty-eight hours sleep before he would feel fully alive again, but within about six hours the telephone rang.

Crunch let it ring three times, then yanked the telephone under the covers and fumbled the receiver to his mouth. "Yeah."

"Crunch?"

"Who?"

"Is this Captain Crunch? Nick Cruschenctuwitz?"

"Who is this?"

"Kurt Crane."

"Who?"

"It's me. *Kurt*. Sixth man, 1969 Posse. The 'Mad Bomber.' If they'd had a three-point shot back then I'd have scored another thousand points."

"Kurt?"

"You all right, coach?"

"I didn't think you would call."

"Hey, I said it wouldn't be easy. I didn't say it would be impossible."

"You found Jerome's dental records?"

"Sort of."

"What do you mean sort of? What are you telling me?" Crunch sprang up out of bed and paced the floor in his boxer shorts. He tensed the muscles in his face and tried to sharpen his senses.

"I have the name of his dentist—Jerome Straughter's dentist. Dr. Roland Rice from the Medicare & E-Z Credit Neighborhood Dental Clinic on West 125th Street."

"Great. That's great. Kurt, I underestimated you. You're my man in the clutch."

"Wasn't I always?"

"Yeah, I guess so. Except for that diving chuck you took against Iowa with ten seconds still left on the clock while Freeman Cook was wide open in the lane...."

"Say, who's doing who a favor here?" Kurt asked.

"Like I've always said, it took guts to put the ball up like you did. It was a high percentage shot. You got a bad break. You were hacked! Those Big-Ten refs are like fuckin' bats in striped jerseys."

Kurt laughed. Crunch laughed.

"Did you talk to this Dr. Roland Rice?" Crunch asked.

"He knows the situation."

"Does he have any X-rays of Jerome's mouth?"

"He says he does."

"Is he gonna cooperate with us?"

"Conditionally...."

"What does he want? Free tickets to our home games? He's gonna fly in from New Jersey to see us play at the Corral?"

Kurt laughed.

"Would he settle for an official Posse warmup suit?"

"No, he doesn't want anything like that."

"What *does* he want?"

"Maybe you better call him yourself, Captain Crunch."


IT WAS ALREADY after noon as Crunch waited on the line for Dr. Roland Rice to finish crowning someone's molars.

Crunch turned on the television and searched for ESPN. He found a wrestling telecast in which two six-hundred-pound men—one wearing a G-string composed of two knotted live snakes—embraced, rolled around, and tried to cannibalize one another.

Crunch turned it off and walked to the window and opened it. The hum of the street soothed his nerves. A building was being erected across the street. Trucks hauled loads of pinkish red bricks. It seemed like everything in New Jersey was made out of this pinkish red brick. It was the color of pale, tired lips.

"This is Dr. Rice," a voice resonated from the telephone.

"This is Nick Cruschenctuwitz. Call me Crunch."

"What can I do for you?"

"I need Jerome Straughter's dental records."

"Oh, you're the gentleman...."

"When can I come get 'em?"

"Is Mr. Straughter still alive?"

"I hope so," Crunch said. "He's gonna have a hell of a time bringin' the ball up court if he's not."

"Yes, well, usually when police request dental records, someone has been murdered."

"Yeah, well, I'm not the police. I'm a basketball coach, and I'm here at Princeton University. I've found Jerome, but he's got an alias, so I'll need to prove it's him."

"Has he seen a dentist under this alias?" Dr. Rice asked.

"How should I know?"

"Can you find out?"

"I don't know. Why? Wouldn't your X-rays still

207

prove it's him?"

"Mr. Crunch, Jerome Straughter has not been to our clinic in over six years."

"What are you saying, Doctor? Are you saying his teeth might have changed that much?"

"He may not even have any teeth, sir. When I last saw him he had multiple carious pockets and gingivitis."

"Well, I can assure you, Doctor, that I saw him last night, and I'm pretty sure he still has teeth in his mouth. Now, I have no way of knowing if they're gonna match the X-rays, but, hey, it's a chance I'm willing to take." For a moment, Crunch's mind drifted. He wondered what number Jerome would want to wear.

*"At point guard, the nation's leading assist man, a consensus All-American, and a shoe-in for the John Wooden Award, the team captain of the Four Corners Posse, number thirty-three, Jerome Strrrrraaaaaaaaaateeeeeeeerrrrr!"*

"So, Doc, when can I come by for those X-rays?"

"As soon as you can round up Mr. Straughter."

"What do you mean?"

"You bring me his mouth, I'll give you those X-rays."

"Doctor, you don't understand. I can't do that. I'd need some type of NCAA subpoena to get Jerome out of practice and take him all the way to New York. I'm getting no help from the NCAA—they're still trying to decide which of my testicles to hang me by."

"Sir, I'm really not interested in your personal problems. My concern is strictly with trying to salvage what is left of Mr. Straughter's teeth and gums."

"Hey, Doc, I know where you comin' from. We have a common interest here: the health and well-being of one Jerome Straughter. Which is exactly my point. You think these New Jersey Nets care about dental hygiene? You think *they've* looked at his teeth? He could have root canals and it would be no concern to them. The pros are like that. It's all business and no humanity. At Four Corners U. we treat our players like royalty. They get free dental checkups and fillings and whatever else they need at our on-campus clinic. In fact, that's why I really called you—because our clinic is gonna need his X-rays for their records. Now, whadda you say I wire you some money and you messenger the X-rays—along with a sworn notarized letter attesting to the fact that they belong to Jerome Straughter. I'm at the Garden State Motel."

# 14

## Recruiting Violations

THE MIDDAY PUBLIC BUS was crowded with senior citizens: men dressed for fishing without poles or tackle and ladies with tossed hair the color of lemonade. They were, for the most part, a lively bunch. When Crunch got on, a woman old enough to have given birth to him stood and insisted that he rest his tired bones in her seat.

Crunch, clutching tightly the manila envelope containing Jerome's dental X-rays, tried to relax during the stop-and-go. Cranes and bulldozers lined the boulevards. Detouring cones choked traffic. For a while, Crunch read over the shoulder of the man to his right, who was flipping through the latest issue of the *Gastrointestinal Review*, but for the most part he stayed inside his own thoughts, dreaming about Jerome Straughter in a Posse uniform, until the bus belched open its doors in front of the Princeton campus.

The older university buildings in the sparkling daylight reminded Crunch of a castle he'd seen on a postcard his first wife had sent him from her second honeymoon. But there was no time to stop and admire any of them.

Approaching the locker room door of the Jadwin Gymnasium, Crunch saw the large spray-painted sign:

CLOSED PRACTICE.
PLAYERS AND COACHES *ONLY*!

Posted below was a typed statement from the team president. It read: "Due to continuing newspaper innuendo and other irresponsible abuses of journalistic privilege (specifically unfounded, baseless accusations about substance abuse and low morale on the New Jersey Nets), we are forced to take these extreme measures to enable our team a fair chance to prepare for the upcoming NBA season."

"I'm not a scribe," Crunch explained to the muscle-bound fellow in a crowd control windbreaker guarding the door with his fifteen-inch deltoids and his forty-two-inch Louisville Slugger.

"It doesn't matter, sir," he replied. "This a closed practice to everyone."

Crunch held up the manila envelope. "Do you know what these are, young man?"

"Pictures from your bar mitzvah?"

Crunch faked a laugh. "That's pretty funny. These

are dental records. The dental records of Jerome…. That is, *Clauzell*—Clauzell Thomas. It's urgent that I get to him. He has a deadly root-canal disease. It could spread and put the whole team on the DL!"

But the armed bodybuilder was unmoved. "Say, ain't you that guy that killed a referee in Madison Square Garden?"

"Yeah," Crunch said, glazing his eyes with feigned mania. "I become sociopathic when I don't get my way!"

"Maybe you should talk this over with Tony Kitchen," the guard suggested.

Crunch did not want to talk it over with Tony Kitchen. He could still recall a nationally televised San Diego Rockets game in 1970 in which Tony Kitchen, then a player, went up for a rebound and sent four other players—two from his own team—tumbling into the VIP seats.

"About when's the practice going to be over?" Crunch asked, but the security guard refused to disclose such information, so Captain Crunch was left to sit on some damp grass beneath a tree with orange leaves and enjoy the scenery for an indefinite period of time.

About midway through the tedium Crunch dozed off and then awoke to the sound of children. His eyes opened and he saw the boy and girl he'd met at practice two days ago—Gus Anderson Jo's kids.

They were playing catch near the locker room door. A woman watched them from the driver's seat of her tan Cadillac. Not the olive-skinned beauty with them last night. An older lady with red hair knotted into a fist. Despite the luxury of her vehicle, she seemed uncomfortable. She lit up a cigarette and dragged tenaciously.

Crunch hoped their presence meant that practice was nearly over. The sun was beginning to set behind a clock tower. Crunch got up and watched the boy and girl throw and catch—and drop—a red, white, and blue basketball made of rubber. When an errant pass rolled toward Crunch, he picked it up and hand delivered it to the two kids.

"I guess they didn't let you into practice today either," Crunch said.

"We had to get haircuts," the boy said. "Our mom made us get haircuts today."

Crunch turned his eyes on the woman in the Caddy, who in turn looked sharply at the security guard, as if concerned about the strange man talking to her children, though she remained inside the car in a fog of cigarette smoke.

"That your mom?" Crunch asked.

The kids nodded. "She's our real mom," the girl said.

"She made us get haircuts," the boy said. "She says we can't just spend every day after school watching our dad play. She says we have responsibilities."

"But we get to see the game tonight," the girl said.

"Game?" Crunch asked.

"They're playing the Washington Bulls tonight," the boy said.

"*Bullets!*" the girl corrected, hammering her brother in the back of the neck. "Washington *Bullets!*"

Gus Anderson Jo was the first player to emerge

from the locker room door. He scooped his kids into his arms and ran, twirling them toward a nearby baseball field. As they passed the tan Cadillac, the kids waved to their mother, who blew them a kiss wrapped in a puff of carbon monoxide.

Crunch could not suppress a surge of envy as he watched the six-foot-ten father chase his scion around left field, knowing how much those kids loved him.

Crunch wondered when and how the luster had come off his relationship with Todd. Crunch wished to God there was something he could do about it. He'd do whatever it took—if he could just understand that crazy kid enough to know what he wanted.

Meanwhile, he watched Gus—now on his back, the two children falling on top of him repeatedly. Crunch wondered how much longer he wanted to coach—assuming he still had a job or could ever get another one. How much longer would he stay addicted to the highs and lows, to the thrill of crunchtime and the emptiness of post-game interviews. When he was seventy years old—assuming his ticker endured that long—would he still crave the oceanic roar of mass hysteria pouring down upon him from the stands of an arena along with the savage embraces and the blind love of his players?

Soon, all the Nets had left for dinner except Jerome. A word with Milt Powdell confirmed that Jerome was having food delivered to him while he underwent whirlpool treatments on his knees and ankles and got wrapped in a mile of tape in preparation for tonight's game.

Moments later, a red, green, and white Jeep pulled

up and a girl in overalls and a Rico's Pizza cap hopped out. Crunch met her at the tailgate.

"Lovely evening," he said.

The girl opened the door of a compartment that looked like something you might see at a morgue for small animals. She pulled out a steaming flat box and two bags.

"I'll take that," Crunch said.

The girl scoffed. "This ain't no lunch cart. I'm makin' a delivery, jack."

"Jerome Straughter, right?"

"Huh?" she asked, piling the bags atop the box and slamming the back of the Jeep with her foot.

"I mean Clauzell. That's for Clauzell Thomas."

"Who are you?"

"I'm with the Nets. I'm director of public relations." Crunch held out a fifty dollar bill. "Keep the change."

The girl snatched Ulysses Grant with her teeth, then handed Crunch the delivery. "Careful. The bag on the left got a drink in it."

"Thanks," Crunch said. "Oh, and can I have your cap?"

There was a new guard—a man who resembled a bloated Curly Neal—stationed at the locker room entrance.

"Delivery," Crunch announced.

"No shit," the shiny-headed guard said—and Crunch was in.

A long dark hallway echoed his footsteps. The smell of pepperoni gave way to ammonia, which gave way to Epsom salts as he neared the whirlpool room.

216

"You're gonna thank me one day," Crunch said lamely to Jerome as he entered.

"I'll thank you now, pizza man," Jerome said, his view of Crunch obstructed by the thick garlic-scented steam. "But first, I'll pay you."

"It's on me, Jerome." Crunch said. He rested the pizza and accessories on a weightlifting bench and moved close enough for Jerome to see who it was. "Why don't we go for a walk?"

"My name is Clauzell," Jerome said, "an' I ain't goin' nowhere."

"I've got your dental X-rays," Crunch said and slid the manila envelope from under his arm. "They are not the dental X-rays of Clauzell Thomas. Now, do I have to show these to the NCAA? Or have you changed your mind about taking that walk?"

"How I'm supposed to leave? I got a muscle treatment goin' on, man. I got a game tonight!" Jerome swatted the surface of the hot water, splashing Crunch.

"You'll thank me one day," Crunch said—he said it almost as a question.

"What for?"

"Taking care of your dental problems for starters."

"I done already cocked my jaw fo' d'Nets' team dentist. I had enough mothafuckas inside my mouth for now."

"The Nets have a dentist? That's good. Great. I'm glad you got your teeth straightened out. It's something that's been on my mind. I couldn't be happier."

"So what it is I'm gonna thank you for one day, man?"

"For seeing to it that you get an education."

217

"I don't want no education. I don't need no education. If I'm good enough to run with the NBA an' park some real money in my pockets, what I need wit' yo books an' yo teachers?"

"Don't you want to be a well-rounded person?" Crunch asked, trying to sound fatherly. He did not want this to turn ugly. If he ended up forcibly taking Jerome, the kid might refuse to play—or refuse to play well. "There's more to life than basketball," Crunch said. "Just ask your half-brother."

"So how come when you was lookin' at me las' year, you said I ain't had to do no studyin', ain't had to go to class hardly, ain't had to do no learnin'. You said I could play ball an' I could party an' you'd take care the rest."

"I said that?"

"On the phone."

"Hey, even coaches make mistakes." Crunch laughed, then saw that Jerome was in some kind of pain. "What's the matter, kid. Is it your knee?"

No, Jerome shook his head, biting his tongue.

"Should I get the doctor? Maybe you need something for the pain."

"Yeah," Jerome said, and pointed right between his eyes.

"What is it?"

"Ain't no use," Jerome said.

"Tell me anyway. I want to know. I care."

"I'm never gonna see her again," Jerome said, tensing his face against his own emotions. "She gone. Gone from my life!"

"It's that Korean girl, ain't it?" Crunch asked. "The

218

one in the picture at the clothing store!"

"I'm never gonna see her again," Jerome said.

"I understand," Crunch said. "You're in love. Hey, it's an occupational hazard of life. Without love we might as well all be cockroaches—or referees."

"I'm never gonna see her again."

"Don't say that. Have a positive attitude."

Jerome just shook his head despondently.

"Tell you what. You get her to Four Corners, I'll get her a job."

"They won't let her out."

"Who? Who won't let her out?"

"The government. The muh-fuckin' Koreans. They holdin' her on a hair farm."

This time Crunch had to know: "Did you say *hair* farm?"

Jerome reached behind him, into the pocket of a dungaree jacket, and grabbed hold of a tattered envelope. He handed it to Crunch, who slid out a thin, onion-skin letter and read to himself:

> Dear Jerome,
>     I am sorry I did not return to you when
> I said I would. It was not possible. I attend-
> ed my father's funeral, and he had many
> debts. Men took me away and sold me on
> the black market to a hair farm where I
> brush my hair all day to make it grow long
> so they can cut it off and sell it to a wig
> factory in your country. I am very sad to
> miss you and love you from so many miles.
> I do not even know if this letter will reach

you. I am praying that one day we will be together.

Love, Sunny

"Those bastards!" Crunch said.

"Every time…. every time I see a lady in a brunette wig I'm thinkin': is that Sunny's hair? I can't get her off my mind! It's a shame. It's fucked up."

"I hear you, son. I hear you…. There must be some way to get her back."

"Cost fifty thousand dollars to bribe them muhfuckas. Plus airfare, plus a immigration lawyer to get her back into America. Can you understand, Captain Crunch. I need some money!"

"You got it," Crunch said, aware suddenly that his voice was an instrument, was an extension of his brain, which was now reacting on instinct, like a seasoned backcourt against a trapping defense, looking for an opening, a seam, and filling it quickly.

Jerome's face brightened. He blew his nose into a stray hand towel. "What I got?"

"The money. Whatever you need. It's on me. We'll set up a special foundation to win political asylum for women in South Korean hair farms. Your honey will just happen to be our first case."

Jerome smiled. "You would do that for me?"

"Captain Crunch takes care of his players."

"You all right, coach."

"All I want is for my kids to be happy," Crunch said, wondering if Jerome Straughter was aware that his new coach had just committed what was perhaps the most flagrant violation of NCAA recruiting

220

rules—something that might even rival the cumulative violations of the University of Kentucky or UNLV or the speculative violations of NC State.

"This is between you and me, you understand," Crunch said, trying to seem casual so that Jerome would not realize just how easily he could now blackmail his way right back to the New Jersey Nets starting lineup!

JEROME WAS READY to start packing, to abandon the New Jersey pro basketball franchise as enigmatically as he had abandoned the Four Corners Posse.

Crunch, however, had other ideas. He couldn't wait to see Jerome, *his point guard,* play. The earliest departure out of Newark flying anywhere in the southwestern United States wasn't till the next afternoon. So he told Jerome, *his point guard*, to go ahead, play this game, show 'em your stuff—show *me* your stuff!

Jerome played—and he was awesome. He stunned the Bullets backcourt combo and drew "oooos" and "ahhhhhs" from an otherwise sleepy pre-season crowd. Jerome went to the hole with authority; he knifed through the defending Bullets until they looked like lost children. On defense Jerome was merciless. He was a Western Union satellite, telegraphing every pass within a ten-foot radius. His jabbing hands made steals, made Bullet guards pick up their dribble and protect the ball. In transition, Jerome was everywhere, and he was in control.

Jerome dominated the first half of the first quarter and did not return for the rest of the half. Tony Kitchen was, no doubt, satisfied with what he saw. No need to waste all his moves on a preseason game.

Crunch snickered to himself, thinking that Kitchen had better savor every magic moment before his point guard went poof!

By the third quarter Crunch grew restless. Too many substitutions made for sloppy play, and the refs all had an itch inside their whistles. Ticky-tack fouls turned the game into a free-throw shooting contest. By the third quarter, Crunch began pacing around the half-filled bleachers. He tried to generate a chant— "Clauzell, Clauzell"—so that Kitchen would put the kid back in and give this game some life, but too many people had their mouths full of hot dogs, beer, and conversation to generate enough volume to reach the Nets bench. By the fourth quarter the only enthusiasm anywhere in the building was Gus Anderson Jo's son and daughter, who Crunch spotted along with the slender olive-skinned beauty. Gus was in the game, and his three fans were going berserk, living and dying with each play. Crunch made his way to the other side of the bleachers and tried to share their spirit.

"You think he'll make the team?" the boy asked Crunch during a time-out.

"He looks good," Crunch said, though in fact the aging Gus looked tired and slow and his shot was inconsistent.

"I hope he makes it," the boy said, his mouth full of crushed ice. "If he doesn't make it," he asked Crunch, "do you think he'll have to go back to Italy or Spain? Do you think he'll be one of the guys that always loses to the Harlem Globetrotters? Is there another team in New Jersey he can play with?"

Crunch laughed.

The boy did not. "We never got to see him when he played in Italy. Mom wouldn't let us visit him. She said it was too far. Our mom doesn't like our dad…." The boy looked over at the dark-haired beauty, then at Crunch. "She's not our mom."

"I figured that," Crunch said.

"Dad says he's gonna retire next year. He's gonna go to law school. That's why he needs to play another season—'cause law school's pretty expensive. He needs to play more before they give him pension money. Then he gets to be a lawyer in New Jersey where we live. But he needs to play another year. That's what he said." The boy was out of breath, eyes pleading with the uncontrollable forces of the adult world.

Crunch kind of wished he hadn't come over and sat down here. He wanted to get up. He wanted to forget he'd ever met these people—but first he needed to say something, to apply a happy face to the situation. "So," he said, "I guess the worst that could happen is you won't see too much of your dad till next year."

"Next year?"

"When he retires." Crunch said.

Play had resumed. The boy, consumed by his anxieties, wasn't even watching. Crunch, wanting to distract himself from the boy's anxieties, did watch. He saw Gus Anderson Jo in the paint on defense, boxing for position. Gus showed surprising power for a guy that age; he'd beefed up considerably since his last brief NBA stint. "Next year…." the boy said in a far-away voice, as if next year were a fairy tale.

"It'll all work out," Crunch said, but even as he said it, he knew that that wasn't the point, and his own voice sounded far away. *He* was talking fairy tale, and the boy was caught up in real life. Crunch tried to cling to the fairy tale. He didn't want to think about his own son, but soon that was all he could think about. Crunch remembered what it felt like when he and Todd stopped living under the same roof—when he became "Uncle Dad" and the twelve blocks that separated them might as well have been twelve continents—when every hour was torturous, when he went to sleep at night, wishing he could conk out for a month or two years or however long it would be before he would stop feeling like a mummy and everything would at least seem to have worked itself out. He had wondered—and sometimes still did wonder—what Todd felt like during those moments. The thought sickened him.

Gus Anderson Jo caught a pass at the baseline. He looked for a cutter. He faked a pass, drew a double team, and then dropped the ball out of bounds.

The boy looked down in anguish. "I don't know. You think he'll make it?" he asked.

"You're so stupid," his sister said, throwing a balled-up pretzel wrapper at him. "Dad's already made it. That's what he said. He said he was traded. He said part of the deal was that he was definitely gonna be on the team. So just shut up and watch the game."

"There," Crunch said, "you see. He's already made it." Crunch wondered how it was that a guy this old and slow could be guaranteed a job. Then he recalled the deal. *Gus Anderson Jo and a third-round pick from three years ago named Clauzell Thomas to go to New Jersey....* Could it be? Could it be that the whole multi-team low-level deal was packaged for the sole purpose of guaranteeing a job to a father who wanted to be near his kids?

Crunch slid over next to the young tanned lady. She smelled of roses, talc, and french fries. "You must be Gus's girlfriend."

"We engaged to marry," she said with an Italian accent and showed Crunch a modest diamond.

"Congratulations. My name is Crunch."

"Crunch? That's a candy bar."

"What's your name?"

"Lucia."

"Pleased to meet you."

They shook left hands.

"Is that true?" Crunch asked, hungering for a happy ending to the boy's story. "Is Gus really guaranteed to make the Nets?"

She laughed. "Guarantee. Is a funny word American has. Gus, he say he like in Milan. He love the people. Not like American people. Always look down at the black person. How you say? Patronize? He is hero with Milan basketball team. Like Bob McAdoo and George Gervin. They were big stars in Italy. Everybody love them. They goin' anywhere, get the best seat in the house, the best wine. In *Roma*, a man give up his parking space for Gus! I love Gus like no other woman ever love Gus. He know that. So is that a guarantee we gonna get married and live happy in Italy?" She lowered her voice to a whisper:

225

"Is these kids. Is something missing. I'm young. I'm Catholic. Gus and me can have many many babies. But no, he got to be near to *these* kids. What can I say? So he call his friend, Ray Meyers, his agent. Says he gotta play one more year inna NBA. He no tell me—he say he already *got* the job before we leave—but I find out the truth. I talk to Mr. Meyers's wife, Julie. She say Gus come back to America an' don't know what he gonna do. Ray tell Gus to go to Indiana for tryout with, how you say…?"

"Pacers," Crunch clarified.

"No, Nick say got to be in New Jersey. Ray say Gus crazy. Gus say that's right. Say 'I'm love my kids very much an' it makin me crazy.' So Ray Meyers say he understand an' he go an' make a deal."

"For Gus to get a spot on the Nets' roster?" Crunch asked, tongue heavy with dread.

"See that boy on the bench? The boy with the beard?" She pointed at Jerome Straughter. "His name Clauzell. If Clauzell make the team, Gus make the team. He's pretty good, that boy."

"Yeah," Crunch nodded. "Not bad. Not bad at all for a player an agent created out of nowhere so he could make a deal…."

"So I guess Gus gonna make this team an' everybody gonna be happy," Lucia said.

Crunch smiled vacuously. His eyes moistened and seemed to fog up—but Crunch could still see; he could see more clearly than ever before. "Basketball's a crazy game," he said, and thought: *It sure as shit is! Ray Meyers is the goddamn hero—and Captain Crunch is the goddamn pimp!*

# 15

# *Basic Skills*

THE FOUR CORNERS CAMPUS was aglow in the morning sun. Warm breezes rustled the rows of coconut palms, which had been imported from South America back when the university was first landscaped. The adobe towers shimmered from virgin coats of veneer; the administration bungalows wore a fresh coat of yellow paint on their jagged stucco. Signs welcoming home Captain Crunch hung from telephone and electric wire poles at all four campus entrances—Colorado Boulevard, Utah Drive, New Mexico Terrace, and Arizona Avenue. A skywriter spread the message—"Bravo Crunch"—across the bright blue horizon, followed by the numbers: "22-4!" That would be the record of the Four Corners

Posse, assuming they won their remaining twenty-two games.

Riding onto the campus, surrounded by the inanimate adoration, Captain Crunch tensed.

"I'm tellin' you, Crunch," Sheriff said, monkeying with the car's air-conditioning controls, "if it wasn't midterms right now, the whole school would be out here cheering you on."

"That's real nice," Crunch said.

"You just wait till this afternoon at your first practice. It's gonna be pandemonium."

"Yeah, I'll bet," Crunch sighed.

"You came just in time, Jerome," Sheriff said, resting his hand on the shoulder of the young man who sat in the backseat, right behind the athletic department driver. Then, to Crunch: "Lasalle Mack's been talking about transferring to Carolina if Dean Smith'll take him." To Straughter: "Not after he runs the floor with you, partner…. You're gonna be one popular dude, Mr. Straughter. You're the campus man!"

The young man forced a smile.

"What's the matter?" Sheriff asked.

"Can't you see he's nervous?" Crunch snapped. "He's gotta pass that SAT or he don't play. NCAA's sending their own monitors to look down his throat so we can't even give him the answers!"

IT WAS WORSE THAN CRUNCH had anticipated. Ten NCAA officials, wearing pinstripes and badges, surrounded Straughter's desk as he penciled in the bars of his scantron. They had frisked him, strip-searched him, and shined infrared lamps all over his

228

flesh looking for any tattoos that might provide answers to the test.

Crunch watched the entire circus. He was indignant. How could *anyone* pass a test under this kind of pressure! But he remained silent—not wanting to provoke members of an organization that was, at the moment, deciding how much to fine Captain Crunch and how long to suspend him from coaching.

"What are we gonna do?" Sheriff asked Crunch, pulling him out of the testing room and into the carpeted hallway.

"About what?"

"The test. How's he gonna pass? The kid hasn't been to high school in two years!"

"I did a little tutoring before we left."

"Answers?" Sheriff whispered.

No, Crunch shook his head, "Just some basic skills."

"What if he doesn't pass?"

Crunch shrugged. He wasn't even, at that moment, thinking about the test or about his basketball team. He was thinking about Patricia Straughter—the one he'd eaten strawberries with. He missed her. He wanted to Express Mail her a one-way airplane ticket to come live with him. He supposed he could call—the phone he'd had hooked up would still ring; maybe, after a couple hundred rings, she would answer. But which Patricia? What if he sent the ticket and the wrong one showed up?

"I've got twenty-five thousand students and alumni coming to the Corral this afternoon for Jerome's first practice," Sheriff said. "What if he's declared

229

ineligible to play?"

Crunch shrugged. "Basketball is a game of drama and heartbreak. You just gotta roll with the punches."

Crunch didn't hang around till the end of the test. He had an important phone call to make, and it needed to be made in private. He stole away to his tiny office and paced the floor searching without luck, for a stray pack of Big Red gum as he rang the number of Dr. Sylvester Buchowzki.

"Hello, Sly?"

"Who's this?"

"Your cousin Mike. I need a favor, Sly. I need for you to come to my team's practice this afternoon...."

"You're still coaching football?"

"Basketball."

"You want me to drive in all the way from Santa Fe for a *practice*?"

"It's a special practice—and I need a special favor."

"Favor?"

"You still in the bone business?"

"I'm retired now. I write orthopedic mystery novels."

"That's great, Sly. You'll have to let me read one sometime. But for now, I need you to come out of retirement. I need for you to set me a baseline screen, figuratively speaking...."

CRUNCH'S PRECARIOUS STANDING with the NCAA was not going to improve. Not today. Though the monitors did not catch Jerome cheating, they were present for the young man's first practice with his new team, and before any players had stepped onto the

230

Corral hardwood, those officials did witness the conduct of the Four Corners Posse fans who filled the twenty-five thousand seats. Every fan, it seemed, had a supply of candies shaped like whistles which they swallowed in honor of their beloved coach. Banners hung from the balconies, announcing such jokes as: "What's the difference between a bucket of shit and an NCAA referee? The bucket!"

The mood surrounding the court was jovial. None of the fans, it seemed, knew that Jerome's eligibility status was questionable.

In the locker room, the Four Corners Posse varsity basketball team, including Straughter and including all but two of the red-shirted freshmen, suited up in silence and waited apprehensively.

At 3:18 P.M., Dean Kimble filled the locker room doorway. His face and toupee were deadpan. He handed Crunch an envelope. "He passed!" Crunch hollered. "Jerome passed! Seven-fifty!"

The team erupted in celebration. If they'd had champagne and Billy Packer, Crunch would have sworn they'd just won the NCAA title.

As this team of destiny ran out on the floor, the crowd chanted, "Jerome…! Jerome…! Jerome…!" and "Lynch Mob…! Lynch Mob…! Lynch Mob…!"

Crunch looked around. Everyone was there—students, alumni from way back, expectant faces, a rumble of anticipation. Yet the place still seemed strangely empty to Captain Crunch. His son wasn't there. Todd hadn't been to a Posse game since two seasons ago when collegiate coaches, including Captain Crunch himself, had commenced trying to recruit him.

231

Three other people who normally would be present for such a momentous occasion were also absent: Bobby Alomar, team trainer, and red-shirted freshmen, Winston Skylark and Tommy Carr. Crunch had, hours ago, sent them to the famous Durango Hot Springs for ligament relaxation and colonic therapy to help drain out the steroids the two youngsters had been given by their high-school coach.

A wireless microphone was clipped to the collar of Crunch's shirt. He could swear he heard his own pores making their little excretions over the PA. Or maybe it was the school band tuning up before launching into the Posse fight song.

Crunch watched nervously as his team formed lay-up lines. The guys were inspired, double-pumped slam jams, reversing no-look back-spinning bank shots, alley-oop over the head stuff—except for Jerome Straughter. He was casual. Just the basic: two dribbles and kiss it off the glass. Crunch could read the minds of the fans: Jerome's holding it back, saving his stuff! During the shoot around, guys were tickling the twine with startling regularity. They were a different team. They were on a mission.

Straughter again was laid-back. He mostly rebounded and tossed the balls back out to the shooters. Just the basic chest pass. But already he had made his mark on this team. Even Aubry Barnes, the anxiety-riddled freshman, suddenly exuded a cool air—and sank his practice shots, despite the huge crowd bearing down at him. Straughter's presence, his mere showing up, had—the sign of a great player—improved all the players around him.

232

His presence even inspired the cheerleaders, who suddenly jumped and flipped and spun like a troupe of Olympic gymnasts. They chanted along with the crowd: "Jerome…! Jerome…! Jerome…!"

Crunch saw a teary glare in Straughter's eyes. The coach walked under the rim and put an arm around his star, cupped his other hand over the wireless mike and whispered: "You're gonna be fine. Everything's gonna work out all right. Don't be nervous. They love you. Being loved is the greatest part of life. Enjoy it. Don't be afraid of it."

"You're all right, Captain Crunch. You're all right."

Crunch blew his whistle. He heard thousands of whistles just like his, blowing in the stands. His voice then boomed over the PA: "We're gonna have a little scrimmage here and see what these guys can do!"

A rousing cheer rocked the arena. Crunch approached his players and divided them up.

Normally in a scrimmage, the top eight players were divided up for the sake of parity. Not this time. Four Corners University wanted to see their highly touted starting five in action together as a unit.

Each player was introduced over the PA by Otis Wagner, the ninety-two-year-old announcer who once was a famed rodeo announcer in Prescott (until he made a joke about a certain steer who somehow knew he was the brunt and attacked the public address booth). First the reserves were named, then the starting five—"La-sallll Maaaaack!" "Clarance WAT-son!" "Jo Muuuuuuuudddddddd!" "Jonny…," and the crowd filled in: "Never-Missssss-A-Shottttt!"—and each player receiving increasingly deafening support,

233

until the final explosion of adoration that showered down upon "Jerome Straaaaaaaa-teeeeeeeeeerrrrrrr!" as he jogged coolly to the midcourt stripe.

Crunch held the ball under his arm, the whistle to his mouth, just like a referee. He played the crowd. He looked up at them all, then pretended to swallow the whistle. The whole place rocked with laughter and cheers. Crunch didn't know where the NCAA monitors were sitting. He didn't care. He savored the moment.

He blew the whistle and tossed the ball to Deontrey Love, ball handler of the second-string team. Trey and the subs worked the ball around until Andre Jones got free for a ten-foot pop. It caromed off the heel of the rim. Joe Mudd cleared the board and flipped the pill to Straughter. The crowd buzzed with an electricity of anticipation. Straughter made a three-sixty turn into his dribble. And then he collapsed on the floor, holding his back.

The Corral fell silent. Crunch swore he could hear each fan's breathing. "Where's Bobby the trainer?" Sheriff hollered, as he and Crunch converged on the writhing body of their point guard.

"He's at the hot springs with Skylark and Carr," Crunch said.

"What do we do, Crunch?"

"I don't know." Crunch left Sheriff and Straughter alone on the floor and told the rest of the team to keep their distance. He ran to the VIP seats and hollered: "I think it's his back. Our trainer's not here. We need a doctor."

"You need an orthopedist, Crunch," said a tall silver-haired man rising from his chair.

"Sly!" It was Crunch's orthopedist cousin from Santa Fe.

"Regular doctors don't know shit about bones!" Sly added.

Dr. Buchowzki tended to Straughter while Sheriff called for an ambulance. The point guard was carried off the court on a stretcher. Dr. Buchowzki and Sheriff accompanied him to the hospital. Crunch stayed behind with what was left of his team. He gathered them at center court. He did not dismiss the crowd— though some fled in horror. He did not detach his wireless microphone.

"I know how you feel, boys," he said to their slumping shoulders and faces—his voice booming throughout the building.

"Is he gonna be all right?" Clarance Watson asked.

"I don't know," Crunch said. "I really don't know at this point."

The crowd, as well as the players, reacted in a mass groan. It sounded like the walls of the building were about to collapse.

"Well, we can sit here and mope about it," Crunch said to the crowd and to his players. "Hell, I could hang myself from the scoreboard over this; I'm the one who was arrested and nearly got killed bringin' him here!—or else, we can regroup and make the most of what we got!"

The crowd cheered halfheartedly. The players just stared at the ground.

"Lasalle, you still want that transfer? You got it. I'll even call Dean Smith and paint you as the hot prospect you *were*—not the quitter you *are*."

Lasalle Mack was a statue of anguish.

"Any of the rest of you want to move on to green-er, snowier pastures? Just say the word. I'll help you. I really mean that. I don't want a bunch of self-pity-ing chumps wearing the Posse uniform."

The team remained forlorn, but their eyes were now on Crunch.

"We're gonna do the best we can with what we've got. I'm gonna coach my ass off, and you—whichev-er of you are left—are gonna play your asses off. And you…." He spun around, pointing at the now stupe-fied pom pom girls. "You're gonna *cheer* your asses off!"

The cheerleaders, terrified of Captain Crunch's wrath, broke into spontaneous, out of synch "rah rah rahs" that sounded like a gaggle of sick geese—until Crunch yelled: "Not now, not now!"

Then he looked up at the crowd. "And you all are gonna come out and support us or don't fuckin' come out at all!"

Nervous coughs echoed from the stands.

"We're gonna be underdogs," Crunch said to his team. "I might have to teach you some slowdown half-court plays, some control-tempo sets, maybe even some of those defensive gimmicks I think are a crock of hyped-up horseshit. Whatever it takes to win some games with or without Jerome Straughter!"

Clarance Watson looked up and muttered, "Yeah, I'm down," and gave Crunch a raised fist salute.

"That's what I need to hear," Crunch said. "I saw you guys warming up. You were psyched. You had the edge, the intensity. You were in that extra-perceptory zone. That's what wins ball games. And you had it—and you can keep it. This practice is not over. Aubry Barnes," he called out to the nervous red-shirt point guard—the kid with the chocolate mousse talent and the nerves of jello. "Take Jerome's place. And I mean *take* his fuckin' place! It's do or die—and I say you *can* do!"

Crunch blew his whistle. The two squads spread the court. Crunch threw the ball to Aubry and yelled, "Play ball!"

OUR SAVIOR HOSPITAL, on East Sitting Bull Lane, was a long rectangular two-story building. The first time Crunch had ever seen it was the night Todd was born. Back then, Crunch thought the place looked like a trailer dipped in ice cream. Now he thought it looked more like a tumor in the sand. The parking lot, a tiny square of brightly painted tar, was much too small to accommodate the vehicles of all the outpatients and visitors—especially with the TV satellite dish hogging six spaces—and thus the desert around it was always scattered with automobiles, and a big cloud of silt hung perpetually around the facility.

Crunch found a reserved parking space belonging to a plastic surgeon named Dr. Melbourne who had been a bench warmer for the 1976 Posse and who, Crunch knew, was on a month-long rafting expedition up the Colorado River. Crunch entered the air-conditioned building and found out where Jerome Straughter was, in a private room on the second floor. The halls were quiet, except for an angry dietician yelling at a pimple-faced orderly that low-sodium meals may not be served with soy sauce.

Straughter was awake as Crunch entered the pine-scented room. Seeing his coach, the young man smiled. It was a crooked smile, spiked at the corners with irony. Crunch winked back, reached into his pocket, and whipped out a winter quarter registration form and class schedule.

"You did good, kid. Real good."

Straughter shrugged. "You're a good teacher."

"Just the basic skills," Crunch shrugged back. "How to catch the ball, dribble the ball, and take a dive."

"And fake a back injury," whispered Dwayne Straughter.

"You just have to want something bad enough," Crunch philosophized. "I'm proud of you, son."

"Thanks, Captain Crunch.

"Don't mention it."

"Remember all that shit I said about you?"

"In the Princeton parking lot?"

"Yeah."

"What about it?"

"I only meant half of it."

"What a relief."

"You're all right, man."

"So are you…, but did you have to get an even seven-fifty on the SAT?"

"That's what you said. You said pass it but don't do too well. You said seven-fifty."

"I meant approximately, Jerome—I've gotta get used to calling you that, and you'd better get used to answering to it…. You could have made it seven-fifty-one or seven-fifty-three."

"I could have made it eleven-hundred!"

"You'll have your chance," Crunch said, heading for the door. "You'll have your chance to show the world what a smart-ass you are."

"Yeah, I guess you're right, Captain Crunch," said Dwayne—alias Jerome—Straughter, though his words seemed hesitant. He scratched uncertainly at his forehead and poured a tiny cup of water into his mouth, using the fluid mostly to wet his lips.

"Not used to the dry air, huh?" Crunch asked.

"Not used to a lot of things."

"You're gonna do fine."

"I don't know," the young man said, fidgeting now with the emergency cord at the side of his bed.

"A little nervous?"

"Truth is, Captain Crunch: yeah, I'm a little nervous. I didn't expect things to be like…. I didn't expect them to be like anything, I guess. I guess I didn't really think exactly about where I was going, except things were going to be better. I guess I was too busy worrying about how well I was going to dribble, shoot, and take a dive."

"You'll get used to Four Corners."

"I feel like I've got to watch what I say."

"You do. Remember, your name is Jerome and you can't wait to get your back straightened out so you can play."

"That's not what I mean. I don't even really know what I mean except I don't feel quite as smart as I did this morning."

239

"That's a good sign," Crunch said. "It means you're a little smarter."

"Do you think I've got what it takes to get through college?"

"You've waited six years, son."

"Yeah, and in a way it was hell—but I got used to it, got used to dreaming. Now that I'm here, I miss the dream. Can you understand?"

"You'll do fine."

"I don't know. I don't know anymore."

"Well, that's probably a good sign too. It's good to believe in yourself, but you need a little self-doubt, some insecurity, like a car needs coolant so it doesn't overheat. I wouldn't say that to my team. In basketball—especially if you're about to go square-off against a powerhouse—ignorance is bliss. But, well, I suppose basketball ain't exactly the same as life. Not all the time anyway."

Dwayne thumbed through the Four Corners University class schedule. His eyes opened wide with curiosity and trepidation. Crunch imagined how imposing such titles as "History of Western Civilization" and "Organic Chemistry" must have seemed to this self-taught scholar who had been alone with just his own brain and the books of a public library for half a dozen years.

"Hey, there's no pressure," Crunch said. "So relax."

"No pressure?"

"Hell no, son. You're here on an athletic scholarship. You're a basketball player. Nobody expects you to crack a single book. Whatever you do, as far as this school and everyone watchin' you is concerned, is gravy."

Dwayne cut a slight grin. He nodded; he vibrated his lips and breathed easily through his nose.

"The only person you got to impress is yourself...."

"I guess you're right."

"...And me. I know who you are, son, and I'm gonna ride your ass. I want some As on that report card or I'll have to kick your ass again," Crunch said, heading for the door.

"You're all right, Captain Crunch."

Crunch reached the doorway and cringed at the empty hallway. Though it was midweek, he felt a Sunday-night dread of desolation right in the center of his chest. It was a feeling answerable only by the likes of a vodka-soaked watermelon or a sleeping pill or a Harlem strawberry.

The young man's voice saved him, momentarily, from his next move: "If there's ever anything I can do."

Crunch turned back. "Thank you."

"I mean it."

Captain Crunch felt like asking about Patricia. When could she come for a visit? And would he get to choose which one? He wondered if there was a way to get the strawberry-loving Patricia to Four Corners without letting the other Patricia know where she was.

Crunch pondered this idea until he was aboard his rebuilt Monte Carlo, challenging the sound barrier on the deserted Quad-state Highway—and when it started to make him crazy, he opened his glove box and retrieved an old jumbo pack of Big Red cinnamon chewing gum. There were six pieces left. They were stiff as popsicle sticks. He pried their wrappers off and slid the little planks of gum between his jaws and gnawed and chomped until they splintered and then became a great wet wad.

# 16

## *March Madness*

IN THE GAME OF PROFESSIONAL basketball, every bad team (and, for that matter, every mediocre team) prays for an impact player. Bill Russell answered Red Auerbach's prayers and turned the Boston Celtics into a dynasty. Wilt made a contender out of every team he played for. Kareem (alias Lew) brought the Milwaukee Bucks out of the dungeon of fledgling expansion teams and led them to the NBA throne. Magic and Bird joined a pair of floundering franchises and turned them into perennial rivals for the crown. Jordan did it for the Bulls, Shaq did it for the Magics—and Clauzell Thomas—alias Jerome Straughter—did it for the New Jersey Nets, transforming them into a bona fide contender. He made the all-star team and was, by the all-star break, odds-on Rookie of the Year favorite.

The Nets, who had only signed him to a one-year contract, made a multi-year, multimillion-dollar deal with "Clauzell" to keep him off of next year's free-agent market. (The deal came just in time for Jerome, whose sudden celebrity had, thanks to satellite television, become known to Korean government officials and thus geometrically escalated all the bribes necessary to get his girlfriend out of a South Korean hair farm.)

It was beginning to look like a Cinderella season for Tony Kitchen and the Nets. They clinched a play-off berth, then earned home-court advantage through at least the Eastern Conference semifinals. Then Clauzell Thomas tore a hamstring and became a question mark for the rest of the season.

The Four Corners Posse also had a season filled with the unexpected. Despite being unable to play, "Jerome" Straughter became the team's inspirational leader. He came to all Posse practices and games—home and away—and, to Crunch's amazement, the young man articulated words of passion about the game of basketball. "Jerome" made his most profound impact on freshman Aubry Barnes, who took his game to another level, maturing into a gutty point guard able to cement the team. The Posse won a respectable number of games. They even stole a last-second thriller from a heavily favored UTEP and rose from a twenty-two-point halftime grave to upset Clemson, which at the time, was ranked number 7 in the nation.

They rehearsed and ran set plays with elaborately

exacted picks and cuts that Bobby Knight might have thought up on his own chalkboard—and opened up the outside shot for Jonny Never-miss-a-shot, who, for the most part, lived up to his name and also became a sharp passer off the double team. Crunch and the Posse designed and perfected ways to pound the ball inside to Joe Mudd and Clarance Watson. They used an amoeba defense, a snake'n'three offensive set, a double-pick railroad-yard transition game. Sometimes, when they had a comfortable lead in the second half of a ball game, the Posse even spread the floor in a four-corners offense that had to make Dean Smith smirk.

"Jerome Straughter" was a team leader off as well as on the bench. He hung out with the other players and steered them away from fights, drug abuse, gang rape, and other hazardous extracurricular activities common to collegiate hoopsters of the latter twentieth century. He also helped his teammates study and tutored them when necessary—and by the end of the winter quarter, the Four Corners Posse basketball team's combined GPA was in the top twenty percent of all NCAA Division-One squads.

This impressed the NCAA upper brain trust, who were surprisingly lenient on Crunch for his attack on Hal Beckett. They settled for a letter of apology and his offer to spend his off-season coaching juvenile delinquents at a drug rehabilitation camp. But Crunch's image as a lunatic still hurt his recruiting efforts—the parents of at least three blue-chip high-school seniors refused to even see him and threatened legal action if he came within one-hundred feet of their sons.

Crunch's new reputation did, however, help him in the recruiting of one young man. The North Carolina Tarheels basketball program, under the assumption that technical fouls were hereditary, reneged on their oral commitment to Todd Cruschenctuwitz, branding the high-school senior as a bad apple and leaving him with nowhere to turn except to his father.

Crunch responded to the needs of his son by pulling strings with the Four Corners Fine Arts Department and getting Todd a music scholarship.

Todd invited his dad to take him out to dinner and then said he would think about playing basketball next year.

TOWARD THE END of the regular season, Patricia Straughter came to Four Corners to visit her son.

Driving to the airport to pick her up, Crunch attacked a sweet glob of Big Red and prayed for strawberries. He had already fixed up his guest room in anticipation—and arranged for "Jerome" to be busy helping Joe Mudd with algebra so as to have some time alone with Patricia in the car.

When she got off the plane, overly dignified in a paisley dress and carrying a Gristedes shopping bag, Crunch was, at first, enchanted.

She recognized him and smiled tentatively.

Crunch took her shopping bag, locked arms with her, and headed toward baggage claim. There, muscling for position alongside the revolving belt, Crunch waited for his mood to swing—to become a self-conscious boy or an uninhibited romantic.

246

Neither feeling ever came. Captain Crunch had no idea which Patricia it was. In the car, they talked about a rude stewardess and the in-flight movie. Crunch drove her to a vacant teachers' housing unit, where she left her bags. Then he reunited what was either a mother and son or an aunt and nephew.

Crunch was sad, but he was also relieved. His life was simpler now. At least for the time being. He would always have the strawberry memory to savor— the same way he would always have his childhood lawn-mowing recollection.

He was happy to be a man with a pair of memories to enjoy.

Three's the charm, he told himself hopefully.

But for now Captain Crunch was a married man— his wife was a game that a man named Naismith invented with a peach basket—and Crunch knew he had better start paying complete attention to that wife because March Madness had arrived.

The Posse fell short of winning their conference, but an impressive late season showing against Arizona put them on the bubble, and, thanks to an untimely loss by New Mexico State, Four Corners got a berth in the Eastern regional of the NCAA tournament field of sixty-four. Captain Crunch, however, could not enjoy the good news, as it came the same day he discovered that Clauzell Thomas (the real Jerome) had suffered a grave hamstring pull that could end his season.

Crunch had followed the Nets and their incredible rise. He had overcome his jealousy of Tony Kitchen and adopted the Nets into his heart. They were his team. Their victories were his. And wouldn't it be grand if Gus Anderson Jo could play out his last year of basketball with the thrill of a championship ring? Now, the Nets's season and Gus Anderson Jo's careers—basketball and law—and his proximity to his daughter and son hung precariously by the hamstring of one point guard.

But Crunch forgot about the problems of Gus and the New Jersey Nets once his own team stepped onto the Philadelphia Spectrum slab and matched up against the heavily favored St. John's Redmen. For the first twenty minutes, the Posse followed Crunch's directions with disastrous results. Clarance Watson got into early foul trouble and Jonny Never-miss-a-shot committed five turnovers. The army of St. John's fans stomped and roared and chanted secular battle cries. With the butts of long plastic bugles, they pulverized an effigy of Captain Crunch, while their team, with inside power and outside speed, pulverized the Posse.

On his way to the locker room at halftime, Crunch could imagine the voice of EPSN basketball analyst Dick Vitale second-guessing him: "Crunch isn't getting enough out of his players…." "He's got to adjust his defense…." "He needs more leadership out there on the court…."

Entering the locker room, Crunch hollered for Jerome Straughter. The team needed some inspiration and Crunch wasn't sure he had any left in him. "Jerome! Where the hell is Jerome?"

"Here I am, Coach." Straughter stepped away from a urinal. He was wearing a Posse uniform, number thirty-three.

"What are you doing?"

"I'm gonna play the second half."

"Are you crazy?"

"A little," the young man said. "Maybe a lot."

Crunch figured the kid was pulling the ultimate inspirational ploy, *a la* Willis Reed, 1970.

Then the second half began—and immediately Crunch realized that this was not Dwayne (alias Jerome) Straughter. This was the *real* Jerome: beardless and scintillating. Possession one, he danced the ball up court like a prize fighter concealing his savage intentions behind a seemingly harmless ballet. He managed, in about twenty-eight seconds, to weave his way through the St. John's offense; not penetrating to the basket, just checking it out, doing a kind of inspection before the demolition.

Then he turned the game upside down. Canned his first three shots, drew the double-team, the triple-team, then skimmed passes to the open Jonny Nevermiss-a-shot for the jumper, the open Lasalle Mack for an off-balance fade away, the open Joe Mudd for a slam dunk, the open Clarance Watson for a monster slam dunk. Jerome's high-gear transitions made the St. John's zone defense resemble a set of bowling pins waiting to be creamed. When Redmen defenders tried to stop Jerome with hard fouls, Jerome heard the whistle, spun out of the contact and into the air, double- and triple-pumped, and then gave the ball a one-way ticket to the bottom of the net for a three-point play.

Halfway through the second half, St. John's lead was stripped to five points. The Redmen tried to spread the floor and kill the clock. Jerome played

249

hide-and-seek with the passing lanes and intercepted the ball three times in a row, each time igniting a fast break that ended in a Clarance Watson two-point earthquake.

The Posse had the lead—and there was no looking back. The St. John's battle cries went flat. Effigies of Crunch continued to surface and get thrashed—only now it was done with malice, not glee. The rest of the game looked like the NBA All-Stars toying with the Chinese Olympic squad.

Nearing the seven-minute mark, Captain Crunch handed Sheriff their playbook and said, "Tear this shit up."

"Tear it up?"

"Tear it up."

"Even the chainsaw rotation set?"

"It's a piece-a-crap, Sheriff. The real playbook is inside that kid's head; it's encoded onto every cell in his entire body! Just like it says in the theory of evolution—it's a hundred years of natural selection, only with God in charge. Hey, I know we're supposed to be the down-to-earth team and St. John's is supposed to be the fire-and-brimstone, but there just ain't no denying it. God has decided to transform the mighty game of basketball and take it to another level—and he's sent Jerome as his messenger!"

Sheriff humored Crunch with a halfhearted nod, then turned back to the court. He saw Jerome snatch a long rebound and wheel up court in overdrive. The Redmen stumbled back in transition but managed to get defensive position. Jerome twirled into the lane. Suddenly, the basketball seemed to disappear; for a full second, no one knew where it was. Even Clarance Watson looked surprised as he rose above the rim, unsure how the ball had become appended to his giant palm, which then rammed it through the twine.

Sheriff tore up the playbook. Crunch helped him. They were speechless—even during time-outs. Crunch just shook his head and smiled in awe and embraced his players. He tried to savor each precious moment of this cage heaven. At one point he imagined the voice of Dick Vitale now raving about the coaching job Captain Crunch had done, the inspiration Crunch must have conveyed during halftime to have so profoundly turned this game around.

In truth, most of the commentary (Crunch would later discover in front of a VCR) ignored the coaching genius of Captain Crunch. Ed Vreeswyk, the color man, spent most of his vocal cords comparing Jerome Straughter to NBA Rookie of the Year favorite, Clauzell Thomas. Tommy Sinclair, the play-by-play man, took great exception: "There's no comparison. This Straughter kid is a schoolyard sensation, but Clauzell Thomas is a proven NBA star!"

The Posse went on to trounce St. John's 96 to 78. In the locker room after the game, Crunch was elated but already felt the inevitable postpartum descent. He cornered Jerome—before the media could get to him—and asked longingly: "Why didn't you suit up for the opening tip-off? I could have had you for a whole game. Maybe half is enough for your mothers, but half just ain't enough for me...."

Jerome shrugged and squirted ice water into his mouth and on top of his head. "I wanted to make sure y'all needed my play." He whistled sadly. "Y'all sure as shit did. Y'all stank the joint up."

"Thank you very much, Mr. Hotshot NBA."

"I'm yours now."

"What are you talking about?"

"NBA playoffs don't start till end of April," Jerome muttered under his breath. "Dwayne gonna grow a beard an sit on the New Jersey bench for me while I's kick some ass for you. Tournament be over in two-and-a-half weeks. Then I'm back in Jersey."

There would be no stopping the Posse. They would lynch any and every opponent. Captain Crunch would take the videotapes of the next five tourney triumphs and put them all on one cassette without commercials and spend the rest of his life watching them. *Yes! Oh, yeah!*

Just to make sure he wasn't dreaming, Captain Crunch sneaked into a back room and flipped on a television set. The Sixers were playing tonight in Jersey. Channel 17 had the action—and as Hersey Hawkins converted a coast-to-coast drive and dunk, Crunch caught a glimpse of Dwayne Straughter—posing as Jerome posing as Clauzell Thomas—having grown a beard. Dwayne was right. They no longer looked that much alike now that he knew them; Dwayne's head was smaller, his features more delicate.

On the replay of Hawkins's one-man fastbreak, Crunch watched Dwayne on the bench in slow motion—trying to look competitive in a sport he neither liked nor understood, trying to seem injured without seeming wounded. Feigning stoicism and succeeding only because no one was really paying much attention to him. Crunch wondered what kind of doctor the young man would make. A pretty damn good one, he reasoned.

"I won't do it," he said moments later to Jerome, cornering him in a shower. "I won't let you play. It's too risky. Too much attention. Someone might figure it all out. You'd be banned from organized athletics, and it might cost your cousin his education."

"Ah, man, don't you wanna win the title?"

"Not that much."

"But I owe you."

"No, you don't. You're paid up, man," Crunch said. "You took me to the zenith of basketball. You wrote the poetry on the hardwood. I had kind of hoped it'd be an epic poem, but I'll take what I got. I'll take my twenty minutes. 'Tis better to have kicked Lou Carnesecca's ass for one-half of one game—and watch him squirm in his latest uglier-than-shit sweater—than to have never kicked Lou Carnesecca's ass at all!'"

JEROME STRAUGHTER (ALIAS Clauzell Thomas) returned to the Nets's lineup (beard and all) after serving out his ten days on the injured reserve list. The vacation was a blessing; it helped him psych up for the season's home stretch and the playoffs, in which his team shocked the world and became the most talked about sports story for three weeks. Superstation TNT's *This Week in the NBA* even devoted a five-minute feature to seldom used reserve Gus Anderson Jo and his fan club of two, which he saw every day after school when the Nets weren't on the road.

During the off season, "Clauzell" would finally be reunited with Sunny, who would soon be Sunny Thomas—Jerome's name having been legally changed. He would purchase two homes in Duchess County, one for him and his bride, one for Patricia Straughter with an acre of land to harvest and eat strawberries. Patricia also made frequent trips to Four Corners. Captain Crunch never did figure out which Patricia it was—whether it was always the same one or they still took turns. Soon he began to forget that there were two of them.

As for the immediate fallout of the Posse's triumph over St. John's and the legendary twenty-minute appearance of Jerome Straughter, the official story went like this: as the result of testing out his back too soon, Jerome reportedly reinjured himself so severely that his entire collegiate career was doubtful.

But he remained a critical part of the team, and the kinetic energy of that one-night—one-*half*—stand with Jerome (the real Jerome) at point guard seemed to carry the Posse through the next two rounds of the tournament before an overpowering Louisville team stopped them in double overtime.

Captain Crunch was bombarded with public and private criticism for having sacrificed the young man's career, his NBA money-making potential, and his general health for one lousy tournament victory.

Crunch took it on the chin. He told the sports media that there was more to life than sports, that Jerome Straughter had been granted the opportunity of a college education and that he could still do great things with his life.

"Why, if he works hard and perseveres, and doesn't feel sorry for himself because he might have had a pro career and if he goes to class and does his homework and really puts his mind to it, who knows? One day, he might even be a doctor!"

# THE FEVER

## BY JAMES NEYLAND

A serial killer is stalking Hollywood: the bodies of young black women are being found strangled and displayed nude on the hillsides. When Detectives Hamilton Barker and Troy Morris are assigned to the case there is evidence that a pair of killers are involved—and they may be cops. But by the time the fourth victim is found, the pattern changes, and so does the investigative team's assignment from headquarters. Suddenly Barker and Morris find their efforts hampered by having to take their orders from a computer. As the investigation stalls and more and more victims turn up, Barker decides to buck the new system.

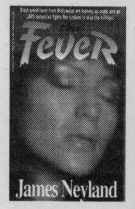